STARFALL

STEALING THE SUN: BOOK 3

RON COLLINS

SKYFOX
PUBLISHING
Science Fiction

STARFALL

STEALING THE SUN: BOOK 3

Copyright © 2017 Ron Collins
All rights reserved

Cover Image:
© Ig0rzh | Dreamstime.com | Full sun eclipse, asteroid impact

Skyfox Publishing

ISBN-10: 1-946176-04-4
ISBN-13: 978-1-946176-04-2

STEALING THE SUN

includes

STARFLIGHT

STARBURST

STARFALL

STARCLASH

STARBORN

Other Work by Ron Collins

Saga of the God-Touched Mage
includes

Glamour of the God-Touched
Target of the Orders
Trail of the Torean
Gathering of the God-Touched
Pawn of the Planewalker
Changing of the Guard
Lord of the Freeborn
Lords of Existence

Picasso's Cat & Other Stories
Five Magics
Six Days in May

Follow Ron at:
http://www.typosphere.com
Twitter: @roncollins13

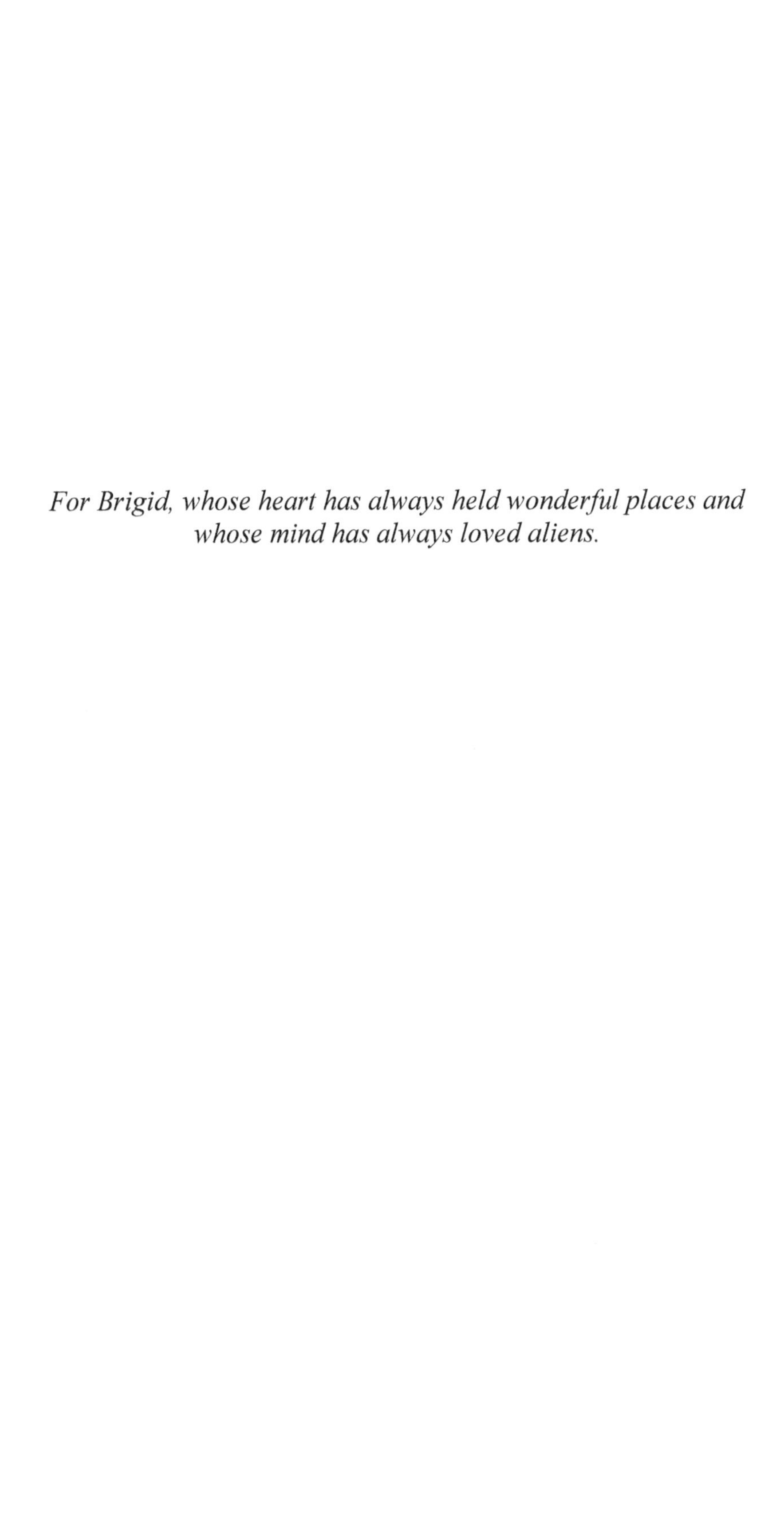

For Brigid, whose heart has always held wonderful places and whose mind has always loved aliens.

Star light, star bright,
First star I see tonight,
I wish I may, I wish I might,
Have this wish I wish tonight.

CONTENTS

INTRODUCTION

As with the first book in this series, the underpinnings of *Starfall* began as a short story first published in *Analog* magazine. After reading *Stealing the Sun* (the original story in the sequence) Stan Schmidt asked me what happens next. The answer came in the form of *The Taranth Stone*, which was a novelette that eventually went on to do well in the AnLab reader polls and be named by CompuServe readers as the best novelette of the year.

That's the thing about this writing gig. You never know where a story is going to go.

Given that *Starfall* is a story set on a distant planet and therefore focused on an alien species, I sat down to write the Taranth Stone with great trepidation.

The problem here is that dealing with different cultures is hard work. Make your aliens too alien and readers have a hard time relating, too human and they don't carry the story quite right. Then there's the planets themselves. The climate, the geology, and the overall ecosystems that these can generate—all these things need to play together just right.

This becomes more than obvious when you sit down to do it.

That said, I admit I love these kinds of stories. The whole idea of alien worlds and characters who are not human is just fun.

Like the corporate world, right?

Can anyone say Dilbert?

I knew you could.

Anyway.

Let me get back on track here by saying that I've occasionally said that science fiction is the most human of literatures. Sure, this sounds great as a sound bite, but I think it's true because every SF story ever told—even those full of pulpy goodness, or *especially* those full of pulpy goodness—is really about what it means to be human.

I hope that *Starfall* is no different.

It's been an incredibly fun story to write. The transitions of the story through its characters, and their relationship to the planet they live on taught me a lot. The idea of time passing, both in the events of the story itself and in relationship to events that we readers know are going on around them in a universe that is so much bigger than these characters can conceive, made me feel such a wide range of things.

That's part of what it means to be human after all, right?

Time passes.

Societies change faster than the people in them want to change, but not fast enough to save them from a certain sense of inevitability.

Through it all, there is always that most human of emotions.

Hope.

Ron Collins
October 2016

PROLOGUE

An umbrella of orange and white plasma blazed over the pod's nose cone as it powered its way through the planet's upper atmosphere. A contrail of gray condensation and brown smoke curled in its wake.

The pod's body consisted of many microlayers of self-aware, nanointelligent titanium, each sandwiched between sheaths of bioactive tissue tightly matched to coolant molecules through quantum links at the atomic level. Together, they acted as sensors and shields, designed, coded, and configured by some of the best engineers in the Solar System to withstand Alpha Centauri A's six-million-degree corona.

Caustic as the planet's upper atmosphere was, comprised of dense sulfuric acid and other corrosive oxides, it was no star field.

The pod's protective shell allowed it to survive entry without damage. As it cleared the upper layers of cloud, its rocket engines—also designed to drive the pod through fusioning material for long enough to complete its mission—sputtered and kicked, suffocating in open sky as the pod glided toward the planet's crevasse-lined surface.

The engine kicked once, then twice, attempting to restart.

The stubby flaring on the pod's fuselage was meant to provide guidance surfaces while deep inside the star. It caught the thick air. Pressures scrubbed speed. The pod lurched downward into the lowest layer of the atmosphere, an oxygen-and-nitrogen-rich segment that held only wisps of clouds and buffeting winds that tossed the pod into a wild flight. The engine gave a final cough, then went silent.

Its velocity was forty kilometers per hour at impact.

The ground shook.

Rocks and dust flew.

The pod rolled and crumpled along a barren landscape, flipping end over end like an errant rock tossed down a hill before eventually coming to rest in an orange cloud of sulfuric dust, wedged between a pair of basaltic boulders at the base of a small mesa. The land here was a vast and desolate desert of what would appear at first, to the pod's creators, to be filled with nothingness, but which upon second, third, and fourth looks might reveal a *piela* lizard here, or a *hoi* root there. If the time was right, perhaps one might even see the graceful form of a *jah* gliding through the air, hunting, watching for that *piela* lizard or even a tiny *kax* stirring amid the hard-packed dirt of the desert floor.

When the dust settled, only the hollow sound of the wind remained, moaning through the harsh ridges of broken ground, while all around the hardy brush clung to the crevasses like the rock was the giver of life itself.

To quadars on the surface of the planet, the pod was a brilliant streak of golden light that burned in an arc across the southern sky, out beyond the One Great Esgarat, and out past the ring of other peaks that gave them protection from the desert. This magnificent javelin of a flare, this ominous omen, this stunning symbol hung in the always cloud-filled sky, brighter than any fire they had seen.

The light dropped jaws. It drew deep clicks from the backs of throats.

Some pointed and spoke to their Families or to clan members. Others ran from it, shielding their vision against its glare. Some spoke of the old gods. Others grew silent, their lips closed, their centrals wide and full of awe.

As the pod fell, the flare left behind a twisted smudge of smoke that faded into the burnt sky. Only those with the sharpest vision could see the dark point of the pod then, as, bereft of its power, it fell further, out beyond those mountains, into the distant zones that all quadarti knew as the lands of the dry and the dead.

Chapter 1

Jafred E'Lar fidgeted as he used his central to watch Ambassador Tacor gather his notes and step down from the podium. Tacor's scuffled footsteps echoed in the half-filled chamber as he traversed the stairs and crossed the floor of polished obsidian. The material of the floor came from the core of the One Great Esgarat itself. It seemed to glow with the life of the quadars who had made it.

The heat was growing late, and all three of Jafred's stomachs were now clenching hard enough he wished he had been able to take an early dinner. He wrapped his six-fingered hands around his own collection of notes and waited his turn.

Tacor, the ambassador from the Kandar clan, was a distinguished Ancient of the Quadarti, named such by the council nearly a full twenty-two-year cycle before—a span during which the rising point of Eldoro, the greater heat, moved across the horizon and back.

Each of those years had a name. This was the year of *kax*, named for a small creature of four legs that was hardy enough to survive on the surface yet prevalent in the underground caves. Next year would be the year of *tal*, named for a slow and thick beast of no little burden that could manage its water well enough to survive in places that would kill a quadar, specifically including the heated pits of river rock atop Esgarat northern volcanoes.

Tacor was hunched over with his years. He moved in slow, lurching steps that spoke of chronic pain. Brown spots mottled his hairless gray skin, which bore both the deep wrinkles of his age and the scarred patterns that the quadars of the Kandar clan traditionally marked themselves with. He had made the long trip here on limited notice, and his message was important enough to him and his Families that he was still dressed in his travel informals, a rugged poncho of root fiber grown in the *hanta* pits by Kandar's Elganjo Family, and a pair of loose-fitted leggings made of animal skin. The ambassador's footwear consisted of sandals laced up over those leggings.

His fatigue was obvious as he wheezed his way to the far aisle to take his seat.

Tacor's commentary had been good. He built a strong case for why the Kandar clan should be given the honor of finding the Light That Fell from the Sky three heats prior.

That was why the council was gathered here.

The quadarti were talking.

They had seen The Light That Fell from the Sky.

They were grumbling, worrying, listening to the words of the priests and the Families and the shyster free-sellers who were always ready to make a profit from any rift in the seam of society. Those words were spreading fear and concern because—in Jafred's mind—all of them, priests, Families, and free-sellers, had come to understand that fear and concern always served to create commerce.

The council had to address the situation soon or the Families would take it upon themselves, and that would create even more chaos which would then cause the council to lose power. In reality, that was already happening. The Families were growing stronger each cycle. He saw that in the way Tacor was given leeway in his arguments even though this emergency session was a closed affair, attended only by the primary members—meaning neither Families nor members of the general public were admitted. Theoretically no information would flow to the individual Families, but Jafred scoffed at that idea. Tacor was given that leeway expressly because his words would be disseminated to the Families.

As the world advanced, the entire idea of the Family caused problems. No one else seemed to see it, yet—no one in the council, anyway. Or at least they wouldn't admit to it. While the value of the Family hierarchy was becoming a routine topic among philosophers and the ranks of scientific thinkers, his fellow council members rarely weighed in on such discussions. His council mates did not consider the ranks of those thinkers to have much value, unless, of course, they happened to employ one of their own.

In that way, the council was no better than the Families.

The council was, after all, about stability.

Business as usual.

The question at hand, however, did not fit "business as usual." Nor did it pertain to research, development, or production. The question before the council was about salvage and retrieval, which followed an altogether different set of guidelines, guidelines that usually fell into the relatively simple category of deciding which Family had lost the material in question, and assigning it back to them. No Family, however, could lay claim to the Light That Fell From the Sky.

So now the council and the three great clans had called themselves to this caucus to decide which Family would be given the honor of undertaking the project, and, therefore, which Family would be provided ownership of said find.

This was, to Jafred E'Lar's way of thinking, a singularly dangerous question.

When Ambassador Tacor reached his seat and had gotten himself settled, Chief Councilor Pelorit spoke.

"The council recognizes Jafred E'Lar, of Terilamat."

Jafred stood, then straightened, pressing one bony hand over the folds of his robes as he clutched his notes with the other. The pressure of more than thirty gazes fell upon him. Those robes were the orange colors of the Quadarti Council, rather than the usual red that marked his original home as the North Slope of the Esgarat.

Despite the air's stagnation, Jafred wore the robes fully covering the plates that ran over his shoulders and acted to regulate his internal temperature. It made him warm, but it showed both deference and concern. It also covered the Terilamat markings of passage that had been branded onto those plates when he was just a whelp.

He hoped his choice set the proper tone.

The chamber echoed with hushed whispers and the clacks of cleared throats as he approached the dais. He closed his central as he climbed the steps.

The podium, offset from the center of the chamber, was made of finely marbled rock, brought here from deep under the mountain, carved by the Lezi Family, and presented to the council as if it were a gift and not an investment in future decisions around the commerce of construction and quarry. It came to his chest, and was polished to a warm red shine that matched that of the floor.

It was carved with the three interwoven triangles that symbolized the council.

Jafred used it as a shield as he took in the entirety of the building.

The chamber was an open space of no little intimidation.

Tall beams of veined stone rose in majestic towers above them, surrounding a rounded floor of community seating with an arching, domed ceiling whose center was open to the sky above. Light from Eldoro, the major heat, burned a smudged ring against the curved section of the eastern wall. From this angle, Jafred could see the entire spiral of polished obsidian that had come from the holy foothills of Esgarat and that had been laid into the floor to much fanfare.

Despite the limited attendance, the air was stale now. Jafred wished for a breeze to offset the tension.

"My friends," he said, his hearts racing as he took in his audience. "As Ambassador Tacor has just said, this may well be the most critical moment in our history. The quadars of our communities care about this. They want to know what we are going to do to find out what has happened. They want to know we are safe.

"In that matter, Tacor spoke of the respect in which the Kandar clans are held, a respect to which we can all attest. He told us of the hardy nature of his clan's Families, and how they have long been able to survive in"—he raised one bony digit—"and *tame*"— he lowered the finger—"the harshest zones of our homeland. He explained how the Kandar were the first to leave the depths of the mountain caves, and he told us of the trust we could place in them if they were given the chore of searching out the Light That Fell from the Sky.

"I commend our friend for his work, and I agree with his commentary wholeheartedly.

"Just as I agree also with council member Gash from the Hlrat clan, who provided us with the ancient myth of Mandrath to remind us of the heroism embedded in the histories told on the Western Slope, and who described the Hlrat clan's own unique histories of exploration and bravery.

"I, however, come from the Terilamat clan. So, you might expect me to have a different opinion."

A proper smattering of something approaching laughter filled the aisles.

"We are three quadarti: Hlrat, Kandar, Terilamat. We come from three different places," he continued, using the laughter as a springboard to give his words momentum. "We think in three somewhat different ways. But we are also each bounded by the great ring of mountains around the One Great Esgarat and each of us is gifted by the same heats of greater Eldoro and lesser Katon. This very council at which we speak now, and to which I and council member Gash have been honored to serve, was founded on the idea that if we allow each of our Families to use their strengths to their best advantage, then these Families would save us all.

"No one can dispute that this idea has worked miracles. No longer do we find any quadar at war with any other quadar. No longer do we see Families of my own Terilamat clan wasting time achieving things the Kandar and the Hlrat clans have already achieved. And no longer do we see the Families bickering over their properties.

"Our people have come together.

"Our Families trade strength for strength under the agreements and guidelines set forth in these very chambers. Indeed, the location of these chambers in the shadows of the One Great Esgarat, equally near each clan, tells of our binding."

Jafred paused.

"Now, however, we are faced with assigning the salvage duties related to this Light That Fell from the Sky to a single clan—or, more exactly, a single Family within a single clan."

He felt the power of the gathering's attention flowing with him.

He heard the sounds of bodies edging up on their benches.

"This is the way of the quadarti: commerce based on this separation of ownership. And yes, it has worked for many years. But I think we have come to the time where we need to look at our reflections and admit that this way has *also* brought us to this point where our Families hold an awkward grip on our society as a whole, where many of us have become hostages against technologies that the most powerful of Families own, where we must pay to use the lands that they dwell upon. This leads me, for example, to commend my compatriot, poor Ambassador Tacor of the Kandar clan, whose travel time was doubled by his need to traverse the high mountain roads when he could not pay the new rate that usage of the lower roads entailed."

Jafred appreciated the startled look on Ambassador Tacor's face. The expression said he had been unaware his predicament was known, and told Jafred he would have to reward his own investigators for being properly covert.

"I must now admit that I find this practice of individual assignment…quaint," Jafred said.

He used his central to focus on his notes as his primaries scanned the faces of his audience, noting the few who sat in stoic disagreement as well as the many who nodded or fidgeted with discomfort at the accusations he was apparently taking so little care to hide. The ideas behind these words were, admittedly, not completely new to the gathering. Fear and distrust of the most powerful Families had been whispered of for years, though only recently had those whispers gotten loud enough to catch the ears of those Families themselves, and only recently had violence sprung up to quell such words. Only recently had that fear and distrust ever been mentioned in council business, even in passing.

He looked up to see Gash and Estant-etan of the Hlrat clan staring with quizzical expressions. Tacor himself sat stoically in his seat now, perhaps among the few who were actually stunned at the direction Jafred was headed. Chief Councilor Pelorit seemed intrigued, and Jafred's own Terilamat cohorts shuffled nervously in their chairs.

"We are no longer the ancient creatures we were when we crawled up from the caves," Jafred said, carrying on toward the climax of his effort, surprised that the words came so easily now. "I think it is time for a change. For the good of all quadarti, I think it is time we take the next step, time for the council to take a more active role in governing our interactions rather than rely upon the Families."

"So I propose a new approach for finding this Light That Has

Fallen from the Sky."

Jafred stood tall, then.

The usual groups of the most active ambassadors wore the usual expressions of committed acceptance on their faces, but this time more of those from the opposite frame of mind closed their primaries in careful thought. He saw the idea falling into place even before he said it, felt the unspoken fear that each of his quadarti associates had felt—fear that one Family and one Family only was going to come out of this session happy, and they didn't know what that might mean to the people of their clans if that one Family did not come from their clan.

He knew then that the bout was over.

From this quick count, and from the feeling of true correctness that came from the depths of his four hundred bones, Jafred E'Lar believed for the first time that, while he would still have struggles to fight, the answer was going to go his way in the end.

"I propose," he said, "that we do it together."

The Expedition

CHAPTER 2

Taranth Melarin wrapped his hand around a stony knob and pulled himself through the tight opening. He could feel the cave breathing here. This vein was the final stage of the climb. He clenched the slab to his left with his knee, then wedged himself into the slot beside him, and dragged his kit up from behind. This he placed in a crack in the stone to his left.

He braced himself as he looked down.

"Through," he called. His voice echoed through the shaft.

"Following!" his friend M'ran Kat'all called up.

Taranth sat back and waited for the others.

He was small for a quadar, which was an advantage he liked. His skin was darkened from years traveling the exposed wildlands outside and south of the Esgarat ring where no civilized quadar would want to live, and rugged from untold expeditions spent mapping the caves of what he considered his homeland. His sweat smelled of the dust that filtered through the crevasses and coated the shaft here.

Yes, he thought. *We're nearing the surface.*

His primaries noted the split in the rock above. A slice of sky showed beyond. His central focused on the path he would take to get there. The triad of his eyes worked together to give him both heat sight and sharp sight, which his brain combined to create a precise mapping of the caverns. This late in the heat, the rocky pathway glowed with uneven heat, something that made movement easier.

He didn't need the image, though.

Like most old trackers, Taranth knew this rock better than he knew the veins that ran across the back of his hand. Unlike the string of his clients that straggled along behind him, he could have made his way up this shaft without any vision at all.

He rested in the hot air.

He coughed, and used the moment to drink from his bladder.

How could anyone with even a single reasonable bone in their body have any desire to live on the surface? Even the breeze that came off the mountains in the evenings and the hours of shaded light from the peaks that allowed for what some called "comfort" couldn't make him have any interest in the surface.

When he was a whelp Taranth had scoured the deserts that lay above with his da and his sisters, mapping its expanse and looking for valuable *kado* root that grew in its shadowed crevasses. He had been so young back then. The entryways to the surface had been exotic. The idea of roaming the flatlands with his da had made his hearts pound so hard he felt the chambers vibrate in his chest.

Now it was just work.

Dangerous work at that.

Taranth licked his lips as he put the bladder away.

He would have to pay attention to the group's water on this trip. These clients were dangerous, too. He should have said no, but M'ran had been insistent and had promised a significant payment. Three times more than the already bloated price Taranth considered asking. So Taranth had agreed to take a batch of Family whelps outside the ring.

He was an idiot.

Perhaps he would eventually be a wealthy idiot though.

After all these years, that might be something interesting.

The plan was to avoid a steep climb under the heats by using the caves to traverse the mountain range, then rise up in the southlands that led to the heart of the desert. There they would create a search pattern, find this Light That Fell from the Sky, and return by retracing their footsteps. It was a basic plan, simple as far as plans go. Taranth had been on such expeditions in the past.

But the plan assumed some level of competence, and this party was a mismatched collection of council members' whelplings, all young and from highly connected Families, all with more education than intelligence. They were twelve "adventurers," four from each clan, handpicked for whatever purposes those clans might have for them in the future.

Before the "adventure" had begun, these intrepid travelers had spoken boldly of the future. They laughed with voices that were too loud, and they joked with each other about which of them would survive and which would be left for the *rela* and the *neantha* beasts to feast on. As if any of these whelps would ever make it through an encounter with either a *rela* or a *neantha*. The closest any of them had ever come to such an animal was in their bedtime stories well before they had come of any age.

They carried their overstuffed packs with vigor on the initial walk, and most continued to wear them for even the first stages of the descent into pathways under the peaks. But as Taranth led the party away from the quadarti mainlands and toward the southernmost foothills of the great ring, and as they descended into the caves, and as the caves wore on and the passages grew more rugged, his boisterous adventurers began to complain. They grew tired of the pace, and they dropped things from their packs, a can of *hanta* bread here or an extra pair of socks there in order to lighten their loads.

Taranth listened to them and shook his head.

"We haven't even gotten to the difficult part," he told M'ran during one of their many breaks.

From the beginning these whelplings behaved as though they were on a simple trek to pick up a shiny trinket, a simple jaunt that would let them fill their journals with stories that would turn them all into heroic figures. He had seen it before. They were here to make their marks on history more than they were here to survive, but nothing in those journals they slaved over would help them deal with what they were going to run into, and no words they could put into those journals would capture the feeling of what it was like to be alone on the dry, cracked lands of the open plains with nothing but the open skies and whatever you could carry to protect you from a world that did not care if you lived or if you did not.

Pah! he thought as he waited.

Only a few generations on the surface and the quadarti had

already lost touch with who they were.

Thinking about the material the whelps had been dumping from their packs along the cave route made him smirk. Any true tracker of the ring would be able to follow their path and get rich doing it.

M'ran wriggled through the hole in the shaft.

His frame was wider and softer than Taranth's. His eyes were purple and wide in the dimness of the cavern. His layer of shirts, now torn and streaked with sulfur stains, were open around the neck to expose the upper reaches of his heat plates.

Unlike the adventurers, M'ran was a representative of the council as a whole. That meant that he was at least theoretically neutral.

Taranth had worked with him before.

M'ran was no explorer, but he was a far sight better than the whelplings.

"We are strung out," M'ran said, leaning his elbow on the lip of the passage and breathing hard with exertion after he pulled himself nearly level to Taranth. "It would be wise to wait."

"What do you think I've been doing?"

M'ran straightened his back.

"I should never have accepted a team of council whelplings," Taranth said.

"Don't complain. If this works out, you'll be known as the guide of the first mutual exercise in history."

"And that brings me such joy."

"It had to be this way, Taranth. Even a free-range relic like you can see that, right? Each clan wants a part of this discovery, and each Family wants a share of the proceeds."

"Proceeds? From a stone?"

"The council thinks this Light That Fell from the Sky is important."

"Thinking something is important does not make it so."

"The holy ones think it's important, also."

Taranth ignored that comment completely. He had lost interest in what the holy ones thought a long time ago. "The Families don't really care," he said. "And they are the ones who would use it to turn profit."

M'ran grinned. "They care."

"Not a single one contacted me."

"We beat them to you."

Taranth focused all three eyes on M'ran, noting his friend's smirk.

"What do you mean?" he said.

But he knew exactly what M'ran meant.

While the council managed behaviors, penalties, and justice between the three territories, the Families controlled business. The Banit Family, for example, owned agriculture. The Waganats lived from developing appliances from newer technology. The Amat'tesh controlled the new field of fuel liquids that were, in turn, providing for new inventions at an alarming rate. He could go on. Garments. Footwear. Tools. Hundreds of products, hundreds of Families—the council arranging for the barriers and assessing claims.

Outside the Families were the parasitic free-sellers who worked alone, and the monolithic Marketelles who worked in tandem with the Families to package products and provide simple commerce for the average quadar, all for a cut of the shares, of course.

Anything for a cut of the shares.

The council, which M'ran was an executive for, had always seen that what was best for the Families was best for the council, so what interested the Families on the scale of commerce eventually became important to the council—just as what interested the church eventually became important to the council on the scale of belief. What happened when the scales of commerce and belief came together was not something Taranth cared to discuss even in impolite company.

Eventually, however, was the key word.

The council was well known for dallying on minutia. Justice, they figured, took time. The council could be depended upon to dither away at least three yields of the moss Taranth grew in his home caves before making a decision on anything of import.

The Families' drive for profit made them move more quickly than the council, and the lack of any particular moral constraint beyond increasing commerce allowed them to do it at all times.

So Taranth had been amazed that the council got to him first.

Until now.

The depth of M'ran's smirk told Taranth that his friend had more information. He widened the skin around his primaries.

"Are you going to tell me what you've done or do I need to leave you and the whelplings alone in the cave together?"

M'ran's smile glowed warm in the coolness of the shaft.

"You, my crotchety old friend of the caves, are the best quadar for this job. I knew that from the minute Councilor Pelorit asked me to manage this. So, the council made it known to the Families that they had hired you immediately after the Light Fell."

Taranth was confused.

"But you didn't even attempt to touch base with me until three heats ago."

M'ran turned his head to the side and shrugged.

"You lied to the Families," Taranth said, fuming as his gut feeling was proven correct. "You directed the council to tell them I was no longer available, so the Families never attempted to contract me."

M'ran raised his hand in a way that indicated guilt.

"That is underhanded, even for a politician," Taranth said. "You cost me a commission."

"The council paid considerably more than your normal fee."

"And the Families would have doubled that."

A clatter came from below. One of the young quadars in the party dropped something that clanked and rattled as it fell.

Taranth shook his head.

"We'll be lucky to survive even a single heat on the surface."

"They're not that bad."

"Pah! They're worse than a den of *kensha* pups before their skin has grown tough. Listen to them. Squawking and waddling behind. They don't know anything. It's like watching a brace of *jah* chicks stuffed into their nests, staring up with open mouths, just waiting for their mothers to fill them to the brim with sandbugs."

"They're just not as comfortable underground as you are."

Taranth craned his gaze upward to the patch of sky that showed beyond the open crescent. "They'll find the desert's worse than the caves."

The thought of Alena crossed Taranth's mind, then.

He saw her at the corner of his perception, her familiar shape with her thin shoulders and her head at just the right angle. He saw her covered in the purple *witze* oils her clan used to protect their skin from the power of Eldoro and Katon when they went to the surface. The image was strong enough to bring him the coarse odor of that oil, and the feel of it, how it had been both gritty and slippery between his fingers as he lathered it onto her.

It had been too long since that had happened.

He pressed his lips together and gave a sigh through his nostrils.

Never do anything for the money alone, she would have said to him if she was here. But he had never been as strong as she was. It was the greatest failing of his life.

"The Waganats will probably beat us to it, anyway," he said as he turned to climb into the shaft above.

"Where are you going?" M'ran asked.

Taranth turned back to the council's executive.

"To the surface."

"What about the rest?" M'ran peered below.

"They will catch up."

"What's your haste?"

"We've already lost half a heat. We'll have to set up our first camp under Eldoro's highpoint now."

M'ran looked vacantly at him.

For a moment, Taranth considered explaining, but it wouldn't serve any purpose. M'ran was—like the others—not used to the desert. He had always lived in the basin where the Esgarat ring cut the weather and where dust storms were fanciful things at best. M'ran didn't have anything in his past to let him know what the desert's heat was really like, or how the burning wind hid up in the shifting layers of clouds, waiting there for so long that it lulled to sleep even the best of trackers before arriving with sudden blasts that kicked up walls of dust in less time than it took to suck in a breath, or with gales that tore through the flatlands with force enough to toss a quadar through the air like a child throws her shaker against a wall.

M'ran lived in the shelter of a surface dwelling, and where food was plentiful and well prepared. He lived off the backs of others, playing out the games of a politician or a businessfolk, rather than working as a maker or living in the old style like a true outsider—like Taranth did and like Alena had—taking only from what the land gave. To M'ran, a harsh wind was one that made funny dervishes spin up in a weed bundle, or made a dust shower for children to run through with their primaries shut.

The desert would teach its truth in its own good time, though.

He would learn. They would all learn.

"The sooner we make the surface," Taranth said, "the sooner we find whatever's left of this Stone of the Sky your council has such interest in."

"And the faster you can get back to your dreary old caves?"

"There is that."

M'ran chuckled. "You are a true ancient, my friend. The quadarti may have crawled from the caves centuries ago, but you would be happier if we still lived half our lives huddled underground like a pack of *piela* lizards."

"At least *piela* lizards know when to be silent."

"Well," M'ran said, focusing his primaries on Taranth. "Once you have your bounty for this jaunt you'll be able to live wherever you want."

"I already do."

Having had enough, Taranth turned and climbed toward the surface. The passage opened as the exit grew nearer.

His nerves calmed as he approached the light.

M'ran had pressed many of his pain points, but he had been right about one thing: At the rates the council was paying, finding this stone from the sky would let Taranth live in peace for a very long time.

It wouldn't, however, be enough to help him forget he was once in love with Alena of the Fex'l Family of the Hlrat clan. And it would never be enough to forget that she was once in love with him.

That was an impossible task if ever there was one.

Chapter 3

Eldoro was edging toward its highpoint as the team struggled to the surface and stood in the baking heat.

Each of the council whelps wore tight-fitting, sweat-soaked garb that was now streaked from the caves. A few wore head coverings against the heat and wind that was now only mildly oppressive, yet was still more than any of the whelps were comfortable with. Four were doused in the purple-toned *witze* oils that marked them as from the Hlrat clan, oils which at their home inside the Esgarat were now considered to be spiritually cleansing and traditional but that here in the desert were still of great value in their more practical role of protecting the skin.

Like most trackers, Taranth carried his own store of the oil for the heats ahead, though his was the natural milky color of the mold and seed compound it was made of rather than the carefully stained concoction the Hlrat required.

He understood tradition. Alena had been of the Hlrat clan, after all.

She had worn her *witze* oils diligently until the end.

It wasn't good to dwell on things that reminded him of her, but the oil struck a chord and made it hard for Taranth to keep from examining the young Hlrats.

Pietha M'ktal, daughter of a fabrics Family, was the eldest. The Tael, Parity, and Gash Families were all represented, the latter being too young to be here but almost certainly having been added to the roster at the request of the whelp's da's da, the ranking diplomat of the clan.

None came from the Fex'l Family, though. Alena's Family.

That was probably a good thing.

No one was included from Taranth's own Melarin Family from the Kandar clan, either. He assumed that was intentional, though it wouldn't have mattered to him. Taranth had not really considered himself to be Kandar for a long time, having broken from both the Family and the clan when he left. Or perhaps that was a mutual decision. It was just as right to say that the Family had broken with him, too.

Everyone gets to make their own choices.

Behind and to the north of the gathering the peaks of the Esgarat ring swept upward into the sky, their rocky surfaces made of orange and red basalt veined with thick lines of iron ore and flint rock. Wiry brown vines and crawlers of other hardy vegetation clutched at the slopes, growing in cracks and pushing their roots into any depression they could find.

With Eldoro so near highpoint, nothing much moved about. But before the rest of the gathering made it to the surface, Taranth watched the final tendrils of flowering buds of the stray *katja* roots close up as they retreated from the heats. Their smell was sharp to those trained to find it—sharp enough to attract the insects and the occasional foraging *kax*, and then use those creatures to spread their seed. The aroma and the sight of their pale yellow petals were a silent welcome, but now the flowers had finished their retreat, leaving the bone-dry plants behind to rasp in the wind until the clumsy footfall of the whelps drowned them out.

To the south the Castanda desert, which was their true destination, stretched for as far as a quadar could see. The sky, as always, was a thick mass of shifting clouds, pale orange now, fading to pink marked with a billowing brown front coming from the west.

A gust of wind whipped up, providing relief from Eldoro's heat as it beat down upon them.

Gis'le of the Family Ombat raised her face to the breeze, closing all three of her eyes and smiling. "That feels wonderful," she said.

The rest were not as charitable. Satrak, a sullen member of the

Waganat Family, merely scowled.

"You are all lucky it is the time of Divergence," Taranth said, scanning them. "With only Eldoro at highpoint, it is merely hot."

"We are not imbeciles," snapped young Hateri E'Lar. "You do not need to lecture us on the effects of Eldoro and his sister."

Taranth focused his central on the whelp, feeling the muscles around the eye grow tense.

The lands of the quadarti had two heats that crossed the clouded sky. Eldoro, the larger of the two, was a bright smear in the clouds that filled the sky and marched in a straightforward path through each heat. Katon, the smaller of the two, moved in a path that was just as certain, but held wilder swings over the cycle.

Convergence, that time when Katon joined her bigger brother in the sky, was the harshest season, a period of hot and bright heats followed by dark nights cold enough to freeze a quadar who was foolish enough to get caught out.

Divergence was the period when the two heats were separated.

At this time of the year, Katon rose late in the time of Eldoro, which meant the fully dark times would be of short duration. But it also meant that the heat, as oppressive as it was, would be slight in comparison to the summers of Convergence.

"Perhaps you know the cycles," Taranth said to Hateri. "But you don't know what they mean."

The whelp's primaries let Taranth understand the youth had the ability to hold his tongue, but was not happy doing so.

"We'll make camp here for now," Taranth said, "and begin the search by the first lights of new Eldoro."

"Isn't it early to pause?" Hateri E'Lar said.

"This is your first heat on the surface," Taranth said. "It is time to learn how to stake our ground while there is time to fail. If any of you grow heat-addled, tell someone, then go back to the caves to cool yourselves. I don't want to kill a council member's whelp before we get started."

A few in the collection chuckled, which made Taranth happy.

His sense of humor often left scars he did not intend.

"We have half of Eldoro left before us," Hateri challenged Taranth again. "And then Katon will help, too. That's a lot of light left."

Taranth's central tightened as he contemplated young Hateri

E'Lar.

The whelp was a gawky male of the Terilamat clan.

He stood there, tall and angular, with his walking stick at a jaunty angle and the wind drumming his loose jacket against his chest. The others of his clan deferred to him because he was the son of Jafred E'Lar, the North Slope council member who had proposed this quest to begin with. Hateri would be an important quadar in the future, and even whelps from the other clans knew it. Several females in the group had eyes for the young E'Lar, and the young E'Lar knew it.

This last realization burned Taranth's hearts.

The world was different now.

Cross-clan relationships were, if not the norm, at least accepted.

The mere idea of a Terilamat like Hateri E'Lar pair-matching with Pietha M'ktal of the Hlrat or Cestral Taler of the Kandar was no longer so unusual. But no matter what Taranth thought, he didn't need these kinds of passions creating problems on this expedition—at least that's what he told himself, and what he would tell M'ran later when the council member called him on his own vengeful form of bias.

Right now, however, all Taranth cared about was that Hateri E'Lar was a renegade vine in need of trimming.

"Do you think I cannot track Eldoro?" Taranth said.

"That's not what I meant."

"Because I learned to track both Eldoro and Katon from my da's da, back when I was a whelp a third your size and half your age."

"I said that is not what I meant."

Taranth raised a finger of both hands and modeled the heats.

"I learned how the two heats play together in the sky even before I made my first crawl out of a cave. How Eldoro marches in his predictable path and how Katon dances around her brother, sometimes together, other times shunning him as if she were the great heat's lover rather than his sister."

The whelp bit his lip. His primaries grew wider as he looked for help from the others, or maybe he looked to see if the others were watching—which they most definitely were, a fact that seemed to make Hateri E'Lar fidget with his walking staff as Taranth came to stand before him.

Taranth broadened his stance into a frame like the thunderous *tal* beast does when faced by a pack of ravenous *rela*.

"My da taught me how the dance is repeated each year," he said, "and how to trace that dance as it moves through the sky in its twenty-two-year cycle—perhaps you've heard of those? I learned to tell shade time at a glance the first time the desert baked my feet, which was cycles before your feet ever existed. So, tell me, Hateri E'Lar, son of the great council member Jafred E'Lar, and possessor of what are most certainly an uncountable number of scholarly records, can you tell me what year of the cycle we are in by the shadow Eldoro casts now?"

Hateri was still silent.

Taranth pointed to a fist-shaped stone at their feet.

"Look at the shadow of that rock. Can you tell me precisely where that shadow will fall at this same time next cycle?"

"No," Hateri finally answered.

"Have you ever seen a *rela* beast up close?"

Taranth raised his arm and let the sleeve of his tunic fall to reveal a jagged scar of whitened skin that ran the distance from his elbow to his wrist.

"Have you ever been so close to one that you can smell the wetness of its breath and feel the orange of its fangs as it gouges you?"

Hateri was silent again.

Taranth's hearts pounded.

"Pah!"

He grimaced and turned away from the whelp, rubbing the back of his hand over his lips as stepped away.

Council members.

Taranth's da's da had been a philosopher. Taranth's da had been a scientist. Philosophers, scientists, and priests for that matter were all the same as far as he was concerned—but council members, whose only desire was to tell him what he had to do, were the worst.

He glanced at M'ran, feeling the stares of the rest of the company as they stood in silence.

"Get the camp set up," he said.

Then Taranth stomped away, heat growing inside him that had nothing to do with Eldoro.

* * *

By the time Taranth regained his calm, Katon had crested to the east.

Eldoro was nearing its end and the cooler winds had picked up, though they were only strong enough to cool his cheeks and the back of his neck where he had left his plates exposed. Still, the winds brought relief from the heats.

He would never understand the allure of the surface.

The twelve young quadars sat together, gasping for breath after working in the desert furnace to pitch their camp.

Taranth examined the work.

The lean-tos were mostly rigged against the steep walls of the largest crevasses the whelplings could find. They had each stored their travel rolls against the windbreak of the rock. They had set a sentry schedule to guard against the snout-nosed *neantha* beasts and muscular and toothy *rela* that stalked the nighttime plains. This close to the mountains, Taranth thought a sentry was less necessary, but practice was important. Three of the team built a water catch to draw liquid from the air overnight.

It wasn't a bad camp, but it wasn't a good one, either.

He considered showing Hiva Hen'tal, of the Kandar clan, how the covering he put up would allow any number of the night critters that were soon to emerge from their shelters to come into his sleeping roll, and how Hiva would be better served to wrap the covering of the whole shelter around to form a floor as the others had done. But Taranth stopped himself. That lesson would most likely cost only a painful sting or two and would be better learned through experience.

Instead, he pointed up the rocky surface where the highest of the shelters had been built.

"Those two are open to the west," he said. "They will have to be redone to keep them safe from the night winds. The others will do now, but you'll all have to anchor them better when we move away from the mountains. Without rock to break its teeth, the wind will shred a shelter if you build it in the wrong line."

One of the collective raised her hand. Gis'le, a female of the Ombat Family and of the Terilamat clan, was small, but sat with an upright bearing that gave her presence a calm aura even though she rarely spoke.

Taranth pointed at her.

"My ma said the winds can pick you up and carry you to the cloud." The worried tremble of her voice belied her calm exterior.

"The wind on the desert can pick you up," Taranth replied. "But don't expect to be soaring with the *jah* anytime soon."

The laughter was wrapped in anxiety. Now that they were on the desert, the gathering was actually listening.

"Your mother's warning is a good one, though." Taranth cut their nervous laughter short by raising his voice. "If we get a true wind—a burning wind—it can pick you up and smash you against rock if you are not diligent. If that happens, I promise you would rather be with the *jah*."

"So," Hateri E'Lar said, scowling, "what do you want us to do, tie ourselves to the nearest boulder?"

Taranth focused all three of his eyes on the young quadar. "What you will do is speak to me as your elder," Taranth said.

The whelp said nothing as wind rasped over stone.

Taranth stepped nearer to Hateri again. His patience was beyond thin.

"I do not have time to deal with disagreement here," he said, waving a crooked finger and ignoring M'ran's silent expression of reprimand. "On this mission, you are my subordinate. So you *will* speak to me as your elder."

Hateri's lips puckered, and he ran one hand over his hip in a nervous gesture.

"I am pleased to accept your complaints about our efforts," he finally said. "And I apologize for my brashness. As your subordinate *on this mission*, what can I do to help you?"

"That is better."

Taranth strolled among the party.

"You'll listen to me," he said loudly to the group. "I'm here because your fathers, your mothers, and your friends on the council know this will be a rugged trip, and that I can keep you alive. Do you understand?"

Ogala, the daughter of council member Tael from the West Slope, nodded with her wide central showing fear. Her primaries looked at Hateri with a sense of excitement, though, and her face, covered with Hlrat *witze,* made Taranth's first heart skip. Ogala's eyes were dark, almost black, like Alena's had been. Though her face was a different shape, the resemblance was more due to the shell of hardening oils over her cheeks, chin, and jawline.

Jasneed of the Parity Family, a male from the same clan as Ogala, shrank back from his seat on a rocky ledge. His oils were also hardening to light blue shells and beginning to flake in the dry air of the surface—though he wore his only over his forehead and bald skull in the way of Hlrat males rather than as a full covering.

Taranth continued. "I was not making humor when I told you that quadarti die here in the desert. Bodies shrivel in the heat. Bones fall into cracks and get sucked back to the soul of the land where we all come from."

He stopped in front of Yanil, who was of the Dareh Family in the Kandar clan, the son of a quadar who did business with several of the council. Yanil had connections. Taranth remembered the whelp's ma from cycles ago. She had been the head of that household. The Darehs were a Family of power when Taranth was growing up. They were whelplings brought up in Families that were forged on the ideas of building new things, unlike Taranth, whose da taught him to keep reverence for lives that came from the stone and the wind.

"Do *you* understand why you need to listen to me?" Taranth said, standing so close he could smell Yanil's anxiety.

Yanil stood taller than Taranth, but his shoulders slumped and he seemed to shrink before him.

"Yes. I understand."

"Good." Taranth returned to the center of the party. "I suggest we do our best to sleep well, then. Tomorrow we will begin our search."

The gathering broke, then.

Taranth stepped toward the horizon where Eldoro had just set and where he would construct his own lean-to.

Low-voiced conversations were carried away in the wind, which Taranth supposed was all for the better. He did not need to hear what the whelps of the council were complaining about now.

Later, as the whelps took to their bedrolls, Taranth climbed to the platform at the top of a formation he knew as Lashto's Break. The jagged slab of rock, nearly twice his height, jutted off into the darkening sky. Old trackers named it for a free-ranger who lived his entire life on the outside of the Esgarat ring and used the break as a primary gathering place for fellow desert-hardened travelers until he just up and disappeared.

That was how most trackers left the world.

They died alone in a land that gave no word of their leaving beyond a body that the creatures and plants of the desert would suck up into themselves in less time than most quadars used to build a home.

The rock that formed Lashto's Break had fallen from the cliffs above before Taranth had been born. He had played here when he was young and his da had taken him on trips. He remembered listening to the wind and the call of animals, watching the night blooms as they covered the surface of the rock with sweet-smelling leaves and light-colored petals. Sometimes his da would teach him to trap *kax* and *piela*. Those were his favorite times as a whelp, trapping in the darkness of Convergence with his da.

M'ran came to sit at Taranth's side.

They dangled their feet over the rocky ledge, a position that should have made Taranth feel young, but instead just reminded him of how old he was. Everything about life made him feel old anymore.

Neither said anything.

Just looked out over the Castanda Desert as it spread to the horizon.

With the dim smudge of Katon as the only heat, the barren land reflected the chalky dome of yellow-gray and brown clouds that were streaked with orange and red. Patches of night bloomers spread their petals to absorb the condensation that was beginning to leak from the air, their fragrance combining with the timeless scent of baked rock in a way that made him feel better. Nearby, rugged *havra* brush and *hoi* root were busy clawing their way into cracks in the stone.

In the distance, dark plumes of rain fell from the highest winds, twisting into burnt yellow columns that disappeared before falling to the surface. The happenstance of perspective made the half-rain appear to mix with ash and smoke that rose from a line of faraway volcanoes.

"Fire rain?" M'ran said, indicating the cloud with his central.

"Yes."

"Good thing we are not there."

"The sky is holding it back anyway."

His words didn't console M'ran, which was good. Fire rain was rare, but when it was cool enough, the orange clouds could open up and drop thin rains of liquid that was strong enough to cut into the bare rock. A smart quadar ran to the caves then, because fire rain could do equally harsh things to skin as it did to stone. As a whelp, he had seen the face of an old plains tracker who had been caught out in such weather. His scars had been deep.

"Hateri will be a powerful ally when he's older," M'ran finally said, his voice as far away as the call of a flying *jah*.

"Perhaps."

"You don't care?"

"I am old," Taranth said. "Why should I care?"

M'ran sighed.

Taranth resisted the urge to spit. Even though it was only Divergence, it was a sorry quadar who let moisture out of his body in the desert.

Instead he ran his hand over a *hoi* root growing in a nearby crack.

"It looks dry and bitter," M'ran said. "Kind of like you."

"This dry and bitter root has saved my life more times than I can tell you about."

"And you thought I was being insulting?" M'ran said.

Taranth laughed, his throat giving an honest clack in response. M'ran was as close to a friend as Taranth had. He was not bad, for a council member especially. M'ran seemed to honestly believe in the idea of combining the clans for the betterment of all, which was different from others who merely wanted to collaborate to extract more commerce in a few specific ways, and considerably different from the staunch holdouts who would rather the entire quadarti population be burned in fire rain than be forced to live and work together.

"I'm not lying, M'ran," he said. "I've lived off these plants more times than I want to remember. They are as sharp and as bitter as you can possibly imagine, and they make my stomachs bind up after a time. But they have saved me."

Taranth took a blade and shoved it into the crack down the length of the root. Then, yanking the *hoi* back and forth, he plucked the tuber out. "Beautiful, isn't it?" he said as he ran his fingers over its length, and finally put it into the satchel he had hooked into the belt around his waist. "Prepared is prepared," he said.

M'ran shrugged. "If nothing else, maybe you can slip it into a pot to give the whelps a surprise."

This time Taranth's laugh was of the full-throated variety.

"Now you're just trying to make me happy."

They listened to the wind for a moment.

"I wasn't lying either," M'ran said. "Earlier, when I said Hateri E'Lar will be quite powerful sometime soon."

"Why should I care?"

"Maybe you shouldn't," M'ran said. He sat silently for a moment, then spoke again. "These whelps are a different breed, aren't they? Full of movement, not so full of thought. Not like us when we were young, eh?"

Taranth grunted. He saw where M'ran was going.

The executive used one finger to pull Taranth's sleeve up far enough to reveal the edge of the scar he had shown Hateri earlier.

"If none of the ancients care about the whelps," M'ran said, "who will teach them the old ways?"

"That is an old trick."

"Sometimes old tricks work."

"Not this time."

M'ran nodded and let Taranth's sleeve fall back. He looked out at a *jah* as it glided on a hot breeze, then he stood, stretched, and crawled off the rock to go back to the camp.

With nothing else to be done, Taranth watched the *jah* glide in the lesser light of Katon's time.

Tomorrow promised to be long.

Chapter 4

The first hints of Eldoro were already coloring the eastern horizon when Taranth spoke to the team the next morning. Given that Taranth rarely managed to do more than doze most nights anymore, this meant he was still tired, unhappy, and in no better mood than he had been the night before.

His wakefulness also meant he knew sleep had been difficult and patchy for most of the others, too.

Pietha M'ktal woke all night with cramps in her legs, and something was giving Hateri's stomachs fits—though the dominant council whelp, as Taranth was now thinking of him, was doing well enough to keep it hidden. All Taranth could say for certain was that Hateri's gastric problems didn't have anything to do with his *hoi* root, which was still resting in his satchel.

The breaking meal was slow.

Packing up camp took longer than Taranth thought was physically possible, and then half the team had to change garb into robes that would breathe better in the heat.

Taranth nearly told them it wouldn't matter—which it wouldn't—but he bit his tongue when M'ran caught his gaze.

Finally, though, they were all gathered and ready to begin the real work they had traveled this way to do.

"From all reports given by the council it seems likely the Light That Fell from the Sky landed to the west and south of this position." Taranth swept his hand away from the mountain. "I suspect this thing is a stone, probably black and burnt—as other things I have seen fall from the sky have been. And if it is like other stones that fall from the sky, I would expect it will be considerably different from others in the area. I also suspect it will be several heats' walk from here, but we will not let such assumptions change how we work. We will gather in groups of two except that M'ran and I will each take a wing on our own. Given the territory, we can put about thirty paces between each group and be likely to find anything unusual."

"How long should we walk, Elder?" Hateri said. He held up the timer he had clipped to his belt.

Taranth bit his lip, unable to hide his horror at the box.

The devices were new. They were small machines being sold through Waganat Family stores. They used gears and other mechanisms to track the precise passage of the two heats, and then represent time in distinct quantities. Only wealthier Families could afford them now, but if the ways of commerce were followed, the Waganats would make them available to the masses once the currency flow began to dwindle.

"We'll head south—away from the mountain—until Eldoro is one-half of one-sixth across the sky," Taranth said, "which, if you pay attention and if you actually listen to the land around you, you will be able to tell without need to barter over useless time boxes."

Hateri glared, but put his machine away.

Taranth ignored him.

"After we walk that distance we'll reassemble, pivot, and return. If we do not find the Stone That Fell from the Sky, we'll pivot again and repeat the cycle, stopping the last pass on its southern tip so that we can extend away from the mountain each heat. That will give us a path six passes wide with each Eldoro."

He had complained to M'ran about taking such a large team, but he admitted now that having more eyes made the search path wider and should reduce the length of the trip by roughly half.

The expedition seemed to understand his commands.

He didn't refresh his warnings about the *rela* beasts or any of the other animals that could make their lives miserable from this time forward, nor did he cover how to report emergencies again. Two times should be enough.

"Searching with that procedure will take forever," Hateri said from his position in the middle of the group. "If we go solo, spread all twelve of us out rather than in groups of two, we can cover twice the ground."

"If we go solo, there will be no one to see you fall into a crevasse and die," Taranth snapped.

Hateri began to reply but, seeing the set of Taranth's expression, apparently thought better.

"Team up," Taranth commanded. "We will begin our search for the stone now."

Voices rose as the twelve began to discuss teams.

"I will assign your teams," M'ran said loudly, quieting the conversation. "The council wants us to work together as Families and as clans. We have an equal number of each clan, so I will assign your match as a member of another clan."

The news was received with neither great joy nor great angst. Rather, it was as if the collective had almost known it was likely to happen. M'ran spent only a few moments making his assignments, which suggested to Taranth that those assignments had been prepared in advance. He wondered if they were of M'ran's choosing, or whether the pairings were another aspect of the council's control.

Did it matter?

Would it matter if Jasneed Parity walked beside Yip Kil, or if he were paired with Gis'le Ombat instead? Did it matter that Satrak Waganat, Terilamat, walked with one of the Kandar clan or the Hlrat?

How could one tell?

Regardless, the teams lined up.

As they started the search, the blot of the greater Eldoro colored the haze of the clouds to the east a dark tone of red.

By the time Katon appeared again and they built their second camp, the entire group was hobbling from blisters and moaning about exhaustion. Without the shade of the mountains, the soil gathered the heat and served to bake the bottoms of sandals. The wind scrubbed their skin raw, even the Hlrat, who were constantly stopping to repair the *witze* oils that cracked and peeled to expose skin.

They complained of strained muscles, and of their water that was warm and stale.

They complained about the sandflies that were invisible until they bit with acidic stings. Taranth didn't tell them that the ache would last for at least a full heat. Let them find these things on their own, just as his da had let him discover them.

They complained about each other.

They complained about Eldoro and Katon and the harsh roots that tripped them when they weren't watching close enough. They complained about the sand that got everywhere.

The desert teaches, Taranth thought as he compared their bickering to the bravado of the whelp's first days. He could not help but take some satisfaction from their misery, though he knew it was wrong to do so.

The farther they walked from the mountain peaks the more the whelps came to understand that their food might run thin, and that the only water they would have was in the packs they carted on their backs and the few drops they could take from their nighttime water catches.

Yet Taranth held them together with his own brand of quietly intimidating professionalism. With a word here or an idea there, the group's suffering became a bonding.

Shared suffering, it seemed to Taranth, was the purpose of life.

When Eldoro rose again, the team was as fatigued as it had been the previous evening, but it got itself ready to go more rapidly than it had the heat before.

The process of picking their way over the ground began again.

Scan south, pivot.

Scan north, pivot.

Do it again.

When Eldoro hit highpoint, they rested.

When the wind blew, they leaned into it. When the dust made it impossible to see, Taranth walked the line to make sure they were all hunkered down safely before finding his own thin depression to weather the storm in.

When Katon appeared, they made camp.

During the fourth heat out, they came upon the pride of *rela.*

Taranth spotted them from his position on the wing.

They were resting in shade created by a meandering ridge of

raised surfaces in the broken ground. A mass of dry brush that grew along the upper ridge of that line extended the shade farther.

Taranth had seen this pack before: five males and eight females, not counting the Dominant, which was the female leader of the pack whose gender changed to neutral after she ascended to her role. They lay on their bellies or on their sides, panting, the short hairs of their burnt orange pelts shimmering in the semi-light of the shadows. It was just past breeding season, and Taranth counted six pups now. The pack would be hungry, but it was also Eldoro highpoint.

The Dominant was watching them.

Taranth felt her calculating the mathematics of the desert.

Was the exertion of a hunt in highpoint heat worth the chances of coming up empty?

Taranth made the whistle and gesture that was the signal for the team to come to a halt, and was stunned to see Hateri E'Lar quickly lean into his teammate, Cestral of the Taler Family. The minstrel's daughter whistled and Hateri used the proper hand signals to direct the entire left wing of the search grid to halt and remain motionless—just as Taranth had taught them.

The rest of the wing came to an immediate stop.

Taranth reached for the knife he kept strapped to his calf.

Held firm in the palm of his hand, his knife was warm and dry like everything else in the desert. His blood pulsed through his palm as he gripped the knife harder. His sense of smell grew sharp, and the skin of his heat plates burned.

They stood like that for several beats—*rela* and quadar staring at each other as the Dominant finished her calculations.

Finally, the Dominant rolled to one side, her back to him.

He gave Cestral and Hateri the "clear" signal, which they passed down the line.

As he slid his knife back into its sheath, Taranth saw that Hateri had shrugged his pack to his side but was shuffling it back to his normal configuration. It told Taranth that the whelp had a blade, too, which was wise. Most of them carried small paring knives as tools, and in fact Hateri had such an instrument dangling from his belt. But his readiness to reach into his pack told Taranth that he was carrying more than a simple working blade.

It made him wonder, but instead of dealing with it there, he motioned the group to move on. Which they did, slowly. Carefully. Making no move that might be seen as aggressive.

He didn't want to be in the area if the *rela* Dominant changed its mind.

Later, when the crevasses that the *rela* had been using were far behind, they stopped at a place where three *havra* bushes grew together to make for a useful shelter. The party sat in its cool shade, sprawled out in much the same fashion as the *rela* had.

"Did you see them?" Ogala said after she chewed on a chip of moss bread and sipped at her water bladder. The *witze* that covered her face was cracked and peeling, but she was smiling. "They were beautiful."

"All I saw was fangs and beady eyes," Gis'le replied. "They made me want to lose my urine, if I hadn't already sweated it out."

"I hope this is worth it," Satrak Waganat added. "I don't want to get eaten out here in the desert."

"They will make for great stories," Cestral replied with a wild grin.

"None of that matters," Hateri E'Lar called out. The group turned their gazes to him.

"What do you mean?" Ogala asked.

Hateri shrugged. "Just that we need to keep our mind on the reason we're out here."

The group grew quiet, each keeping any further thoughts to themselves.

Taranth sat against a shaded rock and sipped from his bladder, enjoying the feeling of the liquid tingling as it passed through his body.

"I thought it was just me," M'ran said from a resting place a short distance away. He pulled his head covering back and opened his shirts to further give his heat plates exposure.

"What's that?"

"Your expression," M'ran replied. "I feel the water all the way to my feet, too."

Taranth gave a closed-lip smile. "There is nothing like being in the desert to teach you what it means to be alive."

M'ran raised his bladder and sipped.

"They did good, didn't they?" he said. "Dealing with the *rela*?"

Taranth gave an affirmative grunt.

His primary stomach grew tighter as he took in the sight of Hateri E'Lar sitting with Pietha of the M'ktal Family. He restrained a grimace at the dagger-sharp gazes that Cestral of the Taler Family was sending them. Taranth noticed that Pietha was enjoying a certain level of attention, and Hateri was enjoying the fact that Pietha enjoyed it. Both appeared oblivious to the anxiety this was causing Cestral, though Taranth was fairly sure Pietha had noticed her competition some time ago.

He drew a breath to help him relax.

The group didn't need that kind of distraction.

"What do you expect," M'ran said to him when he saw Taranth's discomfort. "They are whelps."

"They will be dead whelps if they are not careful."

"Jealousy does not look good on you, my friend."

"Jealousy has nothing to do with it."

M'ran gave his own grunt, but this one carried more laughter than bitterness. "Feel free to lie to me," he said, "but don't do that to yourself."

Taranth scrunched up the crest over his central to show M'ran he didn't have a response. But he couldn't deny the intensity of his jealousy and anger when he watched Hateri E'Lar of the Terilamat openly admire the *witze*-covered face of Pietha M'ktal of the Hlrat, and when Taranth let his gaze go to the scar-lined hands that marked Cestral Taler as Kandar as she wound them anxiously together. Taranth wondered how long it would be before Hateri joined Pietha in her lean-to, or visa-versa. The idea that Cestral might even join them was enough to make Taranth want to spit.

But he did not spit.

Nor did he respond further to M'ran.

When the shadows had moved half a finger width, he stood and got the party back into a line. They moved quickly, and with only a smattering of complaint.

Perhaps, he thought as they began the next leg of the search, this expedition might make it home without incident.

Chapter 5

The chain of whelps was spread out to Taranth's right. He glanced at Eldoro and pulled his robe up to protect his lips from the blustering sand. The wind swirled and hissed around him. Katon had risen for the eighth time since they had begun their search. The ring of the Esgarat far to the north was a small strip of brown on the distant horizon.

Their water supply dwindled.

Frayed nerves and short tempers had served to keep conversation to a minimum, and the only sound Taranth heard was the wind whipping over rock.

And now they trudged through one of the stronger storms that Katon's time had brought since they had left the caves.

There is nothing to find, he thought as he fought the wind. *The Light That Fell from the Sky is nothing but a stone.*

Maybe we should go back.

"Elder?"

The thin voice was almost lost in the wind.

"Elder?" it repeated. A tug at his elbow raised him further from his thoughts.

Yip Kil's eyes were the only noticeable feature visible through her tightly clasped robe.

"What is it?" he said.

"We've found something, Elder."

He followed the whelp as she took him across the expanse of

the desert and into the lee of a small mesa that was almost more of a ledge than a formation. Hiva Hen'tal and Senni Gash were bent over a crumpled mass of broken debris scattered over the floor of a long crevasse that ran alongside the mesa. Gis'le, who had been teamed with Yip, stood back, scanning the whole debris field.

A long, cylindrical object, blackened at one end, was pushed against a cliff of hardened obsidian and wedged at an angle into the space between two boulders. It was huge—several quadars tall.

"What is it?" Yip asked.

Taranth put his hand on the surface.

It was no stone—that much was certain.

It was made of some kind of metal, but smoother than any he had ever felt or seen before. Crotchety ancient or not, even Taranth could admit he felt the excitement of discovery rise inside him.

Word spread, and as he scanned the pieces, more of the team arrived on the site.

"Look at it," he said to M'ran when his friend came to his side.

Taranth pointed to the jagged rips in the thing's outer shell that exposed strangeness on the inside, his eyes gleaming in the reddish light of the dimming of the heat.

"There," he said, pointing again. "And there."

"There's a big piece over there, too," M'ran said, pointing further downwind.

The wind nearly knocked Taranth over when he stepped forward to follow M'ran's direction. His sandals sank into shifting sand as he walked around the mesa. Dust rose up in the current. The smell of sulfur mixed with the odor of trail sweat that permeated every item of clothing the team had.

"Let's break down and get camped," he told the crew.

He held his arm up as a shield against the dust.

The shade here would be a welcome respite, too, assuming the infernal storm ever ended.

The next heat dawned clear, so the party examined the find with exacting detail.

The biggest piece was three or four times Taranth's height, and easily big enough around for him to fit into if the contents of the shell were removed. Its outer crust was a light brown that had been burned black at one end. Parts were crushed and torn away to reveal wiring and boxes and other strange devices on the inside.

"What is it?" Yip asked again.

"How should we know?" M'ran replied.

The rest of the expedition talked in the background, whispering about it, pointing to each other, heads nodding and throats clacking. Only the Waganat stood alone, scanning the device, occasionally touching it, sometimes sighing to himself, other times looking up at the mesa and into the sky.

"I think we'll call it the Taranth Stone," Hateri E'Lar said.

Taranth bristled at the joke until he saw the flavor of the smiles that the name brought to the team. Perhaps he was due a little ribbing. And he realized the team had earned the right to make fun of him. That Hateri used humor this way made Taranth feel like he was a part of the group.

"The Taranth Stone," he said. "I like it."

And the group smiled again.

"It's huge," Hateri said. "We'll never get it back home the way we came."

Taranth clacked his throat in agreement and knelt to peer into the thing's guts. The shell echoed when he tapped against it. It definitely would not fit on the simple skin sleds the group was carrying.

"Other stones from the sky have not been so large," he said, nearly under his breath.

"What are we going to do?"

"I don't know," he admitted.

He had planned to return through the same underground passages they had come from. But this would never fit down the passages near Lashto's Break, nor any other passage he was aware of. They would have to take it back around the mountain and through a pass.

He ran his hands along the object.

"Perhaps we can chop it to pieces."

"I don't think that's wise," M'ran said.

Despite the warning, Taranth pulled cutters from his utility belt, but even the tattered shards proved too tough for the shears, and they were so tiny as to make the effort laughable.

"You're probably right anyway," he said.

The group spent the heat in radial searches, gathering parts that were scattered across the desert floor and bringing them back to the lee of the mesa. Besides being protected from the wind, the area was in the shade of early Eldoro, a combination that helped maximize the yield of their nighttime water catches. Taranth felt the anxiety of the group release as they realized they would stay here for at least the rest of the heat, though personally the idea of staying put made him more anxious.

"I don't like sitting in one place," he said to M'ran as they broke for Eldoro's highpoint.

But what he really meant was that he disliked being unable to answer the most important question on everyone's mind.

As the heat progressed, Eldoro fell toward and then under the horizon. The sky turned bloodred. A patch of green and white desert flowers opened their petals, and Taranth could almost hear the initial scurrying of the *piela* lizards and insects that were readying themselves for the feeding time.

"What are we going to do?" Hateri said as the group gathered amid the wreckage of whatever the Taranth Stone was. Katon was dim in the sky and cast an echo of a shadow over them all.

Taranth drew a breath.

His idea wasn't going to be popular.

"It's obvious we'll have to go overland to get this back. And we're going to need carts and beasts to handle the load. Harshish Point is five heats' walk. We go there, get carts and *tal* beasts, then come back."

"Five more heats?" Hateri said. "Ten, total? And then a trip around the Esgarat? That's what, thirty heats?"

"Probably longer, given that the *tal* beasts will be slow."

"Our water won't hold out for that trip and a return."

Taranth tried not to get angry at the whelp for his direct talk. M'ran had been right about Hateri's effect on the others.

"They will have water at Harshish Point," Taranth said.

The whelp clicked the back of his throat.

"This is what it will take," Taranth said.

Hateri hesitated as if trying to hold his tongue, then let loose anyway. "It's unnecessary is what it is."

"Your alternative?"

"I suggest we go back without the stone. Return the way we came, then ask the council for motor carts to come get it."

"Motor carts?" Taranth asked.

M'ran replied before Hateri could.

"Platforms on wheels that move with the aid of power systems. The Jastari Family built one recently using motors taken from Waganat irrigation pumps."

Taranth shook his head. "There's always something new. Always an easier way. Except they rarely work."

"New ideas often work," M'ran said. "After a time."

Taranth gave a gruff grumble. "The desert will break any machine."

Hateri spoke up. "We'll pay the Jastari to come along on the return trip. They can fix it if it breaks."

"Commerce cannot fix everything."

"A motor cart will travel faster than a *tal* beast."

Taranth glanced at M'ran.

"The motor carts do travel faster than *tal* beasts," M'ran said, not being helpful at all.

The rest of the team looked on expectantly, obviously interested in any option that reduced their time in the desert.

"I don't like it," Taranth said.

"You just don't understand it," Hateri said before M'ran could respond.

Taranth grabbed Hateri by the loose folds of his robe and pulled him close. "I understand you are an insolent whelp who has no idea of his place."

Hateri's central flared with unabashed disdain.

M'ran stepped close by. "Let him go," he said in a low voice.

The wind blew hot on Taranth's face for several breaths before he relaxed his hold.

Hateri straightened his clothing, then stepped away.

"You have not seen the true depth of a desert storm," Taranth said when he finally gathered his calm.

"We've—"

Taranth cut Hateri off with the wave of his hand, and the whelp remained silent.

"I say to you that you have not seen the depths of a desert storm and you want to tell me I am wrong, but I have never seen a motor cart, and yet you still expect me to believe it is a miracle that will save us from pain and hard work?"

The rest of the team stared at him.

"What you've seen on this trip so far is nothing," he said. "Nothing." He waved his hand and turned to M'ran. "The desert will not take to your motor carts. We're going to do this my way," he said, "or we're not going to do it."

Then he walked away.

Taranth needed to be alone.

"Why do you do this, my friend?" M'ran said much later.

Eldoro was long set, and only the thin glow of Katon filled the sky. The team was down for their sleep, and Taranth was taking his turn as sentry. He was glad for the time to sit in the open and hear the sounds and movements of the nocturnal animals. M'ran, standing some distance behind Taranth, was here to relieve him of his assignment.

"Do what?" Taranth replied.

"You're the finest plainsguide there is, Taranth Melarin. But you'll gain no shortage of poor notoriety by shaking the insides from a councilor's son."

Taranth turned to face parts of the Taranth Stone that lay in pieces on the ground. The lesser heat's light painted the burnt portion of the shell the maroon of dried blood. He looked to Hateri's lean-to, knowing that he and Pietha M'ktal had retired there together, and pretending he had not heard the noises they made despite obvious attempts to be discrete.

M'ran stepped to his friend's side. "You cannot change the fact that Alena's dead," he said.

"I know that."

Taranth couldn't say more.

M'ran knew of the troubles he and Alena had suffered between their Families and their clans, and though he was aligned with the council, M'ran wasn't an idiot. He could put three and three together and come up with six every time. M'ran certainly guessed the pain of loss that Taranth felt when he looked at the young whelplings being so free to…cavort.

But Taranth couldn't tell M'ran the deeper truth that raged within him. He couldn't speak the full nature of the dreams that plagued him each night, couldn't give voice to the concern that maybe he had been wrong when he and Alena had turned down the offers of balm and other medications that the Conjise Family had offered to them.

Maybe they had both been wrong.

He could not bring himself to face the idea that Alena might be alive now if they had been willing to try something new. But the medicines scared them both, and they had *not* been willing to try the Conjise's balm.

Instead, they placed their faith in the priests and in the mountains of the Esgarat.

And Alena had grown worse.

Now, standing before this strange not-stone that had fallen from the sky, Taranth could not bear to tell M'ran how on the last night—when her whimpers were so faint and so pitiful, when the pain had grown so bad that she called out continuously through the darkness—that he had finally relented. He could not tell M'ran that in that darkest moment he had lost his resolve, lost his faith in her beliefs, lost his faith in the priests. That he had called the Conjise medicine peddler to administer those roots and other medicines that they had promised could help.

That still she had died before Eldoro had risen.

But that she had lived to see the Conjise arrive.

She had lived to see him remove her *witze* oils and replace them with his lotions.

Taranth would live for the rest of his life with the memory of the expression on her face—an expression that screamed "How dare you betray me" through the murkiest moments of his dreams.

The Conjise Family said it had been too late. The medicines needed time—time that Taranth had not given them. He didn't know if those words were true or not. He would never know, could never know, and in fact, did not ever *want* to know because if a time came that he learned Alena could have been saved, he could not live with that knowledge.

So he didn't tell M'ran that he was afraid his decisions had killed his beloved Alena, or that he could not try Hateri's technology because to see it succeed where his own efforts failed would say that new technologies could work better than the old ways. He didn't say that this knowledge would cause him more damage than he could bear. Instead, he merely retreated to his sleeping pallet in silence, spread it on the floor of the crevasse, and stared at the dark lumps of the thing his group was calling the Taranth Stone.

Taranth decided then that he did not care what the Taranth Stone was, but that he was determined to see it brought to the council by his own sheer will rather than through any of Hateri's beloved technologies.

That was how it had to be.

Chapter 6

Taranth woke with the aftereffects of a dream playing in his head.

He rolled off his bedding and went to the water catch. Each cup contained barely an inch of liquid. Not much, but it would do no good to complain.

The team was still sleeping. Katon was fading to the west, and Eldoro would not rise for some time.

Yip Kil was on sentry duty. She watched him swirl his cup and sip from it.

The liquid refreshed the taste in his mouth.

"What are we going to do?" Yip asked quietly when he sat down on the rock beside her.

Taranth made the huffing sound that requested silence.

The time before Eldoro rose was his favorite moment on the surface.

It had strength to it.

The sound of the wind was touched by the final calls of *jah* and *rela* packs and the more solitary *kish*. If you listened right, sometimes the wind would bring rustle of a *piela* lizard as it raced across pebbles to find its crèche. The air was usually calmer in the pre-Eldoro heat, too, and the skies were often colored with dazzling displays of light. Now, for example, the eastern sky was red and purple with a single blazing streak of gold that curled along the horizon. The heaviest clouds marked the western darkness in a way that suggested turbulence later. He felt a dust storm in his bones.

The Esgarat range was a tiny sliver against the horizon, and Taranth savored the essence of the morning as he and his da had done so many times back when he was young.

It seemed such a long time ago now.

When he was done he turned to Yip Kil.

"Never interrupt a quadar's first moments of the heat," he said, just as his da had said to him the first time Taranth had interrupted him.

"Accept my apology," Yip replied, bending her neck and turning her primaries in proper deference to his age. He saw the scars branded across her fingers that marked her for the Kandar clan, and that matched the old marks on his own fingers. He studied the piercings in her cheekbones and along her primary ridge that marked her for the Kil Family.

Taranth pulled his lips back in a dry grin. The whelp's attitude fit the morning in a satisfying way. She could teach some of the others.

"You asked what we would do," he said. "It's quite simple, isn't it? We will go to Harshish Point and get carts and *tal* beasts."

"But the motor—"

"Motor carts can break in the best of times, true?"

She hesitated. "I've never seen one."

"A desert storm is not the best of times," Taranth replied as if it was the wisest thing said throughout history. "There is no other answer."

Yip flicked a hand upward and clicked her throat to suggest agreement, but Taranth saw she didn't like it.

"We won't do it," Hateri said from across the crevasse.

The young quadar had just come from his lean-to. Both his central and primaries were focused on Taranth. A streak of blue *witze* spread across his cheek and down his neck. Behind him, Pietha M'ktal crawled from Hateri's blanket.

"I'll return alone, Elder," Hateri said, his accent on the term *Elder* as thick as the oil smeared over his face. "And I'll still beat you back here."

"Good luck," Taranth replied, standing.

"I'll do it."

"It's not easy to find Lashto's Break unless you know what

you're looking for. And if you can't find Lashto's Break, you won't find this mesa."

"I will still return first, Elder."

Movements came from the sleeping team—the tone of the conversation having clearly woken them as much as the volume.

Taranth gazed at the whelp.

"Then go," he said. "Go back to your da and to his council, and live your life however you feel it should be lived. That's been your goal from the beginning, so go. If you *do* somehow manage to retrieve these stones that are not stones, then good for you. But you should know that your da personally asked me to lead this search because I am the only plainsguide alive who knows the desert like a fourth heart."

Taranth saw the shock on M'ran's face.

The council's executive thought he was the only member in on the negotiation and that he had brokered the deal through their friendship, but that had never been true. The elder E'Lar had plans, it seems. He had come along after M'ran and made the offer considerably better.

"When I declined," Taranth continued, "he begged me to reconsider because he said the falling light could not be retrieved without me. *He* is the one who convinced the rest of the council to pay a fee few wanted to pay. So if you leave, and if you do see your da again, be certain to tell him of his mistake—and when you tell your da that he was wrong, I recommend you use the same tone of voice with him as you have been using with me."

Hateri glared. "Perhaps I will."

"Then, Hateri E'Lar, I suggest you pack your roll and go with good speed. While you are traveling alone, I also suggest you avoid movement at highpoint."

Taranth turned to the rest.

"In the meanwhile, the rest of us will also need to prepare for a trip. Harshish Point is a good hike away, but at least we can travel at a normal pace rather than at a searching saunter."

When the group left a short while later, Hateri E'Lar was with them.

CHAPTER 7

Heat rising from the baked ground curled in the air as Taranth and the group drew closer to Harshish Point. Eldoro beat on the back of their necks. The wind tore into their already raw skin. Though it was too early in the evening for its flowering, Taranth could smell the essence of *katja* root in the air.

To Taranth, for whom comfort was a clean floor and a cool cave, Harshish Point would be the hub of culture.

The others were of different minds.

A series of sand squalls had turned the five-heat walk Taranth had promised into six heats, and then seven. Yanil Dareh twisted a knee two heats in, so he walked with a gnarled stick in one hand and leaned on Yip Kil with the other. Three others suffered from heat sickness, their skin growing orange and their centrals sometimes roaming in random patterns.

As they neared Harshish Point, they were weak, sore, and too tired to do anything but argue with each other.

Not that Taranth could blame them.

He felt exactly the same.

To call Harshish Point a village was giving it too much credit.

The settlement was a sawgrass-rough outcropping of civilization built into, under, and around the isolated knob of a remote formation that was almost, but not quite, a mountain. It was home to a handful of outsiders, free-range quadars who made their lives in the wild deserts far to the south of the Esgarat. The scorched plains surrounding it were mostly level and barren. The crease it sat in was not quite a valley, instead more of a curved twist in the desert that might have been formed as the wind whipped around the rocky formation that gave the place its name.

The quadars here used the almost-mountain as a shelter from the weather. They used the radial ridges that sprung from the ground around it to defend themselves from the occasional bandits and raiders who thought they might benefit from the stores of goods that everyone knew were there.

Its inhabitants were a couple hundred animals of constantly shifting type, and an equally shifting collection of quadars, maybe fifty at any one time—each with a dubious love of the surface and a demonstrated ability to scratch life out of almost nothing. A few permanent living spaces had been carved into the bare rock, but most were built of gnarled wood that had been carted here from the cities on the backs of *tal* beasts or on the backs of quadars themselves, then put up again and again and again as the wind ripped them down.

The numerous fissures torn into the landscape gave entrance to a twisted tangle of caves where the quadars often stored items of value—or perhaps just of great secrecy—and where they retreated when the burning winds rose up too harshly. The wider caverns were used as cool shelters, bunks, and storage areas, while the smaller breaks and channels often grew the luminescent molds and slimes that desert quadars used as food, dye, alcohol, and for any other purpose they could devise.

The area had an endless supply of the *katja* plant, whose roots anchored themselves into rock, whose leaves crawled over flat sheets of rock each morning to drink spare molecules of water from the air, and whose fruit was a staple of the quadars here. The root reproduced so rapidly that harvested sheets would yield again a mere handful of heats later. Without the *katja* so close by, Harshish Point would almost certainly not exist.

But it most certainly did exist.

As such, Harshish Point was a place that lived on the random nature of free commerce, a place where desert people could rest and catch up on news while they bartered for the few necessities of their lives. Occasionally, L'rdent himself—the gnarled-up quadar who had built the first of the Point's hovels so many years ago, and who was so strongly tied to this place that it was impossible to conceive of the idea he would ever leave—would make a gathering, sell some fermented *katja*, and tell stories.

Taranth spotted the first of the sentries sitting, motionless, at the brush line along the ridge of the sharp cliff-line that led to the settlement proper. The sentry's garments blended with the hardy thicket to make it nearly invisible. Once Taranth picked that one out, though, he saw another was at the peak of a raised stone on the opposite side of the pass.

Normally he would have set up camp earlier, but he thought they could make Harshish Point by the time the great heat was gone from the sky. The lookouts proved that assumption correct.

"What are we going to do?" M'ran said when he, too, saw the quadar atop the stone.

"What do you mean?"

M'ran pointed to the sentry. "He is probably with weapon."

"I would hope so," Taranth said.

"You would hope so?"

"And I would expect the same for the others."

"Others?"

"Two more."

M'ran scanned the area around him. "I still see only the one."

"The second is on the running ridge," Taranth said, biting back a caustic remark while M'ran scanned the ridge to confirm Taranth's comment. Taranth was as sore and unhappy as the whelplings were, but this was not the time to let M'ran's babbling get him distracted.

"And the third?" M'ran said once he had found number two.

Taranth smirked. "Does not want to be seen."

M'ran gazed at him. "You're guessing."

"No. I am certain there are three, but I cannot find the third so I'm saying the third doesn't want to be seen."

"He could ambush us."

Taranth wiped his arm across his forehead to forestall his comments until he could say them without disdain.

"That the third can hide properly says these quadars understand the desert," Taranth said. "That the third is *choosing* to hide now rather than showing force says they are interested in us rather than concerned about us. I would like to think this is because they have seen me at the lead of our little group, though that could just be me being wishful."

"You're saying they respect you?"

"I'm saying they have been watching us for some time, and have not brought up a show of force."

M'ran twisted his lips, then looked over his shoulder to scan the team.

"Don't worry," Taranth said. "I have no intention of getting the council members' whelps killed."

The anxiety in M'ran's expression had already served to put the twelve on edge. They clearly knew how close the end of this leg was supposed to be.

Hateri rushed to catch up, limping on sore legs, his lungs wheezing with the effort.

"What's happening?" he said.

Taranth raised the fingers of his bony hand and slowed his steps to let the stragglers catch up. He didn't miss the fact that Hateri E'Lar and Pietha M'ktal had started this leg of the trek together, but were now separated. All of them were separated, in fact. They needed their space, it seemed. None of them wanted to speak to each other. *That's the desert doing its teaching,* he thought. Drawing its heat and its dust into your lungs for long enough makes anyone question the nature of their existence. Seeing how life clings to rock, and how life adjusts to the land around it was enough to make any quadar question what it meant to be alive. And those questions are always better faced alone. No one exited the heated plains without taking a quest inside their own minds.

As they collected themselves, most dug into their water bladders to take what little liquid remained in them. They had taught themselves to ration their stores by now, some sipping a few drops at a time, others going as long as they could between full mouthfuls. Taranth was pleased.

"We have visitors," he said, making an obvious display of pointing out the sentries. "They are almost certainly armed, so I need us all to keep walking. Stay near me, but spread out enough that they can see who we are. It is important that you not present weapons." He looked at Kip, then at Hateri. "Not a knife. Not a stone. Not a throwing needle. Nothing. The Harshish need us as much as we need them, but they will defend what is theirs before asking questions—so our challenge now is not to give them reasons to ask questions."

The conversation made several eyes grow wide. The team had been prepared for heat, thirst, *rela* beasts, and the rest of the problems presented by the free-range, but the idea of quadarti aggression did not fit their preconceptions.

"We didn't come out here to deal with packs of belligerent renegades," Hateri said, confirming Taranth's read.

Taranth's face flushed. "I have been here before. They will know me. Follow my instructions and we will be fine."

The whelp's gaze narrowed, but he was too weary to argue.

"Are there any other questions?" Taranth said.

The gathering was silent until Ogala spoke up.

"What if the people there are no longer the ones you know?"

Taranth grunted. It was a good question, or at least close to a good question. The right question would have been "what if L'rdent has been usurped? What if the entire settlement was now overrun by renegades?" Secretly, he judged M'ran lacking for having not asked it.

"Word travels. I would have heard rumors."

It was not a complete lie, anyway.

Words did travel, but Harshish Point was a hub, and a hub could be managed. Words would flow through it or *not* flow through it because L'rdent knew how to mold a message and put it on the wind, and because he also knew how to make it known that passing words he did not wish passed could result in misfortune. Even the wildlands were not immune from politics, it seems. But any quadar strong enough to take control of the Point would know how to manage such things, too. Nothing is forever, and L'rdent was even more ancient than Taranth. The relative riches of Harshish Point would eventually bring an adversary great enough to take the village.

Yes, eventually.

So, while they could certainly be walking into a thorny situation, Taranth needed the whelps—and M'ran—to be calm, so the half-lie that said he was not concerned was required.

Taranth took the lead again, smiling to himself as he heard

footsteps getting in line behind him. The whelps had no option but to follow him.

The party kept a steady pace as they crossed the open pass.

Taranth made their progress obvious so the Harshish sentries could make their assessment. A flash of light reflecting from a knife came from the brush line, followed by another from the hill.

A final movement came from the sand ahead of them, and the third sentry appeared to rise up from behind a heat wave that shimmered in the last rays of setting Eldoro, his forehead visible first, then the rest of his face and his shoulders appearing before finally the entirety of his body was visible.

As the third came forward, the other two sentries weaved their way down the slopes to the right and left, revealing themselves, but retaining the high ground when they stopped. Both carried bows that were already strung, and both flashed blades that hung from belt loops at their sides.

Taranth halted his team.

The third sentry approached from ahead. Taranth hoped he would recognize the quadar, but it was not to be.

The third was wiry, draped in loose-fitting clothes that flapped in the new wind and had been made of orange-brown cloth fabricated from fibers of the desert scrub. His primaries were drawn hard on Taranth, his face covered in colorless *witze* that had been applied long enough ago that it was flaking off to reveal skin marked with dark patches. His hands were wide and knobby, all twelve of his fingers oddly spaced in the way that showed that as a whelp the quadar had been subjected to the peculiar practice of hand-tying—a process where young quadars' hands were bound over progressively larger rocks so that their bones and their flesh were formed to be both wider and longer. These larger hands were supposed to make for better climbers.

The process had always seemed grotesque to Taranth.

So much pain, he thought, for so little value. But who was he to judge what was right for another?

"I am pleased to find another who knows how to hide in the heat," Taranth said. "It is a skill few understand."

"What are you here for?" the Harshish sentry said.

"These whelplings and I serve no threat," Taranth said. "We need shelter and rest, and we wish to buy beasts."

The quadar examined them all. His grin was an orange-toothed taunt.

"You are an old thing. The others look like they would trip over a knife."

"As I said. We provide no threat."

"That much is certain."

"I would meet with L'rdent to renew our storytelling," Taranth said.

The words had the desired effect on the quadar, but before he could reply Hateri E'Lar spoke up. "All we want is to rest."

The sentry used his central to gaze Hateri's way, focusing on the whelp with such intensity that Hateri actually shut his trap. The sentry's primaries, however, stayed on Taranth. "You cannot control the whelp?"

Taranth grunted. "Perhaps we can leave him with you as tariff for our passage?"

The quadar grinned.

"You are a hired hand, then," he said.

Taranth indicated the correctness of that statement with a movement of his hand.

"They say you can choose your fares," the sentry said.

"They also say you can starve," Taranth replied.

It was a common phrase among plainsguides, and the quadar's use of it brought them immediately together.

"I think we can let you pass as long as you promise to take him with you," the sentry said.

Everyone smiled, then.

Everyone except Hateri, anyway.

CHAPTER 8

That first night, while M'ran and the whelps took refuge in cavern spaces, Taranth stayed above the surface, watching Katon cross the sky and dip toward the horizon. He wanted to be alone, he said. He wanted to sit in a quiet space and drink water. He wanted to watch over the land they had crossed over these past many heats.

But that was not true.

He thought about that as he pressed himself into a dark slot in the west-facing cliff that gave him cool shade. Eldoro had set long before, leaving behind Katon's thin, almost shimmering glow. The lesser heat was still before its highpoint and its light cast a shadow out in the distance before him. The grounds of Harshish Point proper lay in a depression below him, and for a few moments he watched as two quadars worked to repair a portion of their water catch.

He sat back and laid his head against stone.

The liquid he drank filtered through his body with a tingle that made his skin sensitive to everything it touched.

He thought about the truth of why he wanted to be out here rather than in the caves with the rest. The only useful part of getting old was that he had gotten better about lying—even to himself. But, of course, that was too harsh, also. What he had gotten better about was not lying, but in holding two or more ideas in his head, and working with whichever was most convenient at the time.

He could, for example, tell M'ran that he was happier on the surface, and he could make the executive believe it because he could pull up his memory of Alena, and he could use her love for this place and this moment as if it was his own. He could push away his own discomfort with the heat, and shelve his desire to be surrounded by stone—or at least he could put that desire into a side-stage of his mind like his body stored away pools of blood in his third heart for use later—and he could, instead, bring up the memories of sitting with Alena right here at Harshish Point or at any one of the other outposts they had traveled through when she was alive.

He could remember the feel of her head on his shoulder, and the taste of *witze* oil on her kisses. He could recall the feeling of the world being so incredibly large when he sat next to her in Katon's twilight.

"It's my favorite time," she said to him the first time they were here together. She pointed to the brown and the red troughs of clouds that shifted in the sky, and talked about the light of Katon as the lesser heat rode her excruciatingly slow and seemingly haphazard dance across the sky.

He remembered Alena's touch now, sitting in the calm of the crevasse and looking out over the horizon as wind carried waves of dust to the west and as heat waves warped the view.

The desert was their place, he thought.

The "outside." Away from Families and their dislike for each other.

The outside was the only place Taranth and Alena could be together, so it was where he brought her. And Harshish Point was the first place they had come. It was here that he had sat with her on that first evening. Here that he understood exactly what they were doing together.

So this is why he stayed above the surface that first evening.

Because he was thinking of Alena again.

Or, of course, he could instead pull up memories of those quadars of his own Melarin Family and his own Kandar clan who attacked him for his interest in one of the Hlrat clan. He could choose to remember the bitter voices that called him a traitor and a turncoat. The hissing names that his own Kandar called him: Westie, *witze* breather, or worse. Considerably worse. And he could remember the feeling of rocks pelting him as he came from the eastern slopes to her western homeland of the Hlrat.

He closed his eyes and saw Hateri and Pietha together—but mostly what struck him was how unaffected the rest of the whelps had been, how simple it had seemed to the collective of the whelplings to see the two of them pair-mated, as if mixing of the clans was normal. As if they never considered the idea of picking up stones to separate the pair.

He had met Alena only three cycles ago. Just over sixty years, but it could have been six hundred. How different might his life had been if they had been born in the time of these whelps? Where might they have lived? What might they have done?

Sitting here, Taranth wished he hadn't taken this charter.

He wished M'ran hadn't put Alena's name so directly back on his mind.

He wished he had not seen Pietha M'ktal sliding out of Hateri E'Lar's lean-to or the smear of her *witze* oil across Hateri's face, and he wished he had not been so pleased to see them separate.

He wished…he wished he could stop thinking about her.

But that, too, was all a lie.

At the end of it all, the pain of being on the surface was worth every minute of remembering her.

"There you are!"

The voice startled him enough that the back of his hand hit the stone of the crevasse beside him. It was M'ran, up from the caves.

"I'm sorry," M'ran said as he gathered his thin field robes and sat on the dusty ground outside the crevasse, his hood pulled partially over his head. When he was settled, he handed Taranth a skin that smelled sharply sweet. Taranth drank from it and was not surprised to taste root wine. He handed the skin back and wiped his hand over his lips.

"Not a worry," he said. "I was just thinking too loudly to hear you coming."

"What about?"

"Time, mostly. Time, and things that happen in it."

"Easy to get sentimental when you find a place to rest, eh?"

"I suppose that's it."

Taranth waited until M'ran drank from his skin again before continuing.

"What is it you want?" he asked.

M'ran gave him a sideways expression.

"Don't pretend you didn't come out here for a reason."

M'ran scoffed, but settled in. "You need to be careful of the whelp," he said.

"Hateri?"

M'ran nodded. "He's a leader."

"He's an obnoxious braggart."

"I understand you were, too, in your first cycle."

Taranth grumbled.

"You should have seen him below."

Taranth glanced at M'ran with his central, waiting for the executive to continue.

"Several of the team still want to go home underground," M'ran said.

"They would never make it."

"That didn't matter to them. They are tired and sore. Their feet are bloodied up, and their bellies hurt from the diet we've got them on. You have to remember they are not used to this."

"It takes no effort to remember they've grown up soft," Taranth said. "Do they think they are the only ones to feel the wrath of the desert?" He arched himself against the rock, then uncrossed his legs to stretch them across the ground. "My back hurts, too. My legs are bunched like knotted rope. The plates on my blades are still warm with the heats and my shoulders burn with the ache of the walk."

M'ran took in a breath of patience through his nostrils, then let it out. "Did that feel good?" he said.

Taranth's laughter was both dry and caustic.

He reached for M'ran's skin and took another drink, a full mouthful this time, a gulp of liquid that went down with an acidic pain that did somehow serve to make him feel better.

M'ran took his wine back, and merely put the topper on.

"You think of yourself as an ancient who holds onto the old truths," M'ran said. "You see yourself holed up in the caverns of the old cities built down in the cool rivers that flow in the deepest depth of Esgarat's ring. But these new quadars of the Families see you in different ways."

"They see a bitter old quadar who lives to walk the caves,"

Taranth said. "What of it?"

M'ran shrugged and squinted into the harsh distance, then took another swig of his skin.

"You're going to get clobbered at that rate," Taranth warned.

M'ran's eyes gleamed in Katon's darkening rays.

The aura of contentment that settled around the executive annoyed Taranth even more for the fact that M'ran was right. Taranth did not miss the fact that M'ran ran called the party quadars rather than whelplings. He had been around too long to miss the point that M'ran was making about their status.

"So, tell me about the whelp," Taranth said. "What did he do with these rabble-rousing mates of his?"

M'ran grinned. "Got them settled."

"Wonderful."

"Brought them water, and got *katja* root for the ones sick from the heat."

"Sounds like he'll make a delightful nurse when they get back home."

"He listened to them complain, and didn't say a word."

"That's useful."

M'ran drew himself up. "Don't be like this."

Taranth grumbled.

"The Taranth Melarin I supported at the council was more willing to see the heats of truth rather than use sand to blind himself."

Taranth grimaced. "Go on."

"After the rest of the party began suggesting they leave on their own, Hateri told them stories."

"About what?"

"About the Quadarti. About their Families. Times they had gotten together for events, and how they found games to play while their Families worked out issues. He answered them all with talk about why they were here, about how they were trying to work together for the first time, and then finally about the Taranth Stone, of course. Its purpose. What it might mean to get something of that nature back into the Esgarat for study."

As M'ran paused for a breath, Taranth's anger faded to something closer to embarrassment.

"It was interesting to watch," M'ran said. "As a professional politician, you know? I almost didn't believe it myself, but he was very good. He told a thing about Eldoro and Katon, and wove in a joke about their parents on the council. And as he did it, he wondered what this 'stone' out in the desert could be. A message from one heat or the other? Something from another quadar someplace far away?"

Taranth interrupted. "Sounds like he has a touch."

M'ran nodded. "I think that after this, the entire group would rip a passage through the Esgarat Mountains if he would ask them to."

"Even the Waganat?"

M'ran chuffed. "There is more to Satrak than you might think," he said.

"I think he's too silent for his own good."

"Maybe. But he comes from a Family of not inconsiderable power, and one where to question the head is to be chastised."

"Which means?"

"It is a life that teaches one to silence questions."

"Thank the old gods for miracles, I guess."

"I don't think the old gods had a lot to do with it."

Taranth gave his travel partner an inquisitive gaze. "There's more to this, isn't there?"

"More to what?"

"You came here for a purpose, and I can't imagine it was to tell me things I already know, or to brag about a whelpling's ability to twist his friends about his fingers."

A grin came over M'ran's face.

"I cannot pull truth over an ancient's gaze, eh?"

"What is it?"

"We are going to speak with L'rdent tomorrow about acquiring the *tal* beasts."

"Yes. That's what we're here for."

"We need to include Hateri in our party when we meet L'rdent tomorrow."

"No."

"It's the right thing to do."

"It's insane. There's no way to know what Hateri E'Lar would say if he spoke with L'rdent."

"The group needs to feel like they are participating."

"Don't cast your diplomat's cloak around me."

"It's true."

"Pah!"

"But that's not the only reason we're going to bring him with us."

Taranth bit back a groan. He didn't want to hear what M'ran was going to say next because it was going to be about the aspect of this mission that annoyed him most.

M'ran said it anyway.

"If the Families learn there was such a negotiation, and that they were not a part of it, they will be very unhappy."

The words hung invisibly in the air, no different from the curtain of dust that the wind blew up in the distance. That curtain settled in the light of Katon's highpoint, but the words remained in Taranth's mind. He did not like politics, but he was not stupid. If he would have thought harder about this before, he could have predicted it.

"All right," Taranth said. "He can come. But he cannot speak."

M'ran smiled and gave Taranth's knee a bit of a shake.

Taranth grimaced.

Then M'ran stood up and smoothed his robes as they flapped in the gentle breeze.

"I'm going to get some sleep before our session," he said.

"I will see you at first Eldoro," Taranth replied.

When M'ran left, Taranth turned his gaze to watch the last heat waves of the night rise up into the horizon.

Chapter 9

"I cannot sell you what I have already sold to another," L'rdent said. He held a stone bowl beneath his nose, rolling it in gentle circles to disperse the aroma of the smoldering root that burned in it.

L'rdent did not own Harshish Point.

He was not its ruler, and did not claim to govern it.

He was never elected to a position of power so much as he had always given so fully to the land that other quadars had taken to deferring to him. They had been doing this for so long now that no one challenged him.

Whatever history lay behind his position, his opinion was respected and his word taken with the same certainty as the fact that Eldoro and Katon would bring along shifting of clouds and colors. The ancient quadar now controlled every aspect of this collective, and the rest of the quadars here were fine with that. His word was the closest thing they had to law.

Harshish Point had been that way forever.

To the whelplings their guide was old flint, but Taranth himself could remember L'rdent as a figure of excitement as far back as when his own da had brought him to Harshish Point. He was a true ancient, shriveled into a tangle of rough skin and dry bones that Taranth thought the wind might pick up and smash against the desert every time he stepped outside. His breathing sounded like a desert wind, dry and rustling on both its intake and its exhale. The skin at the folds of his eyes and lips were fleshy and lined, but his fingers were bony and the knuckles of all six fingers of each hand were as bulbous and hard as deep-rooted *hoi.*

He was still sharp, though. Sharp and brilliant.

L'rdent's primaries may have been baked to the deepest brown, but his central was still crystalline blue. And right now those eyes said L'rdent could do nothing for them, and those hands said he was not willing to discuss the topic further as, quavering, they placed the smoldering bowl back to its place at the center of the table that stood between himself, Taranth, M'ran, and Hateri. Like almost everything here, the table had been chiseled of bare rock, but unlike everything else its top had been polished to the smooth glow that Taranth had complimented so sincerely when they first entered.

Good stonework was a gift.

The meeting was being held in L'rdent's chamber—which was a rounded area that legends said the quadar had single-handedly carved from the cliff when he was younger. He had wanted the place to be his, said those stories, so while others made their homes in the natural depths of the caves and by building shacks and lean-tos above the surface, L'rdent had taken pick to rock and, using only the sweat of his own effort and the smelted metal of the tool, had gouged this place straight out of the land.

This, some philosophers of the outside said, was what kept L'rdent alive. He was tied to the land now, they said. It was impossible for the old quadar to die. Taranth had his own opinions on that, but when he looked at L'rdent's withered shell of a body he could not totally discount the idea.

The room was oval in shape, a single space sectioned in ways L'rdent used to manage different pieces of his life.

A straw and bramble bed lay to the left of the entryway. The center of the floor was marked with concentric circles such that when the door was opened, shadows of Eldoro and Katon fell at places that told the story of the heats' movements. Taranth knew from experience that L'rdent used the center mark of this map as a place of meditation, believing as so many did that it was a position of power, and that the old gods had looked upon his place with relative peace for so long in part because he had remained true to the old ways.

The table where they sat had been placed to the room's east.

Taranth squirmed on his bench.

The door was closed behind them, and the fact that the chamber had no other opening gave Taranth a sense of being trapped that he never got while out in the free caves. The strong odor of burning root, and the fact that he was here with M'ran and Hateri added to the feeling of being out of place. He was not one who enjoyed the politics of barter, and the addition of Hateri in particular made the conversation feel like a competition.

They exchanged pleasantries and stories about the desert for several moments before L'rdent had finally broached the subject of what they were here for and Taranth asked him the price on *tal* beasts.

This was when L'rdent had said he could not sell the animals.

"You have already sold them all?" Taranth replied.

"I have."

"We need only three."

Taranth had assessed the settlement earlier, strolling past the corrals and open ranges in the span of pre-Eldoro, and counted easily fifty head in and around the settlement.

"I have made word to sell them all."

True gloom came over him. The hollow sound of wind and the scratches and thumps of movement along the paths outside L'rdent's chambers were audible in the distance. If L'rdent gave word, it was as good as having already laid trade.

"To who?"

"Galen of the outer north. Her quadars are coming now to drive them home."

Taranth had dealt with Galen, and had no great love or happy memory of the process. She was a free-range quadar of similar stature as L'rdent, but less open and less willing to find common places. She came upon her lack of flexibility honestly, having come from the Festia Family before taking her independence from the Terilamat clan. Her control of the outer north was made as much by intimidation as anything else.

Taranth fought the urge to ask what Galen had paid for something more than fifty *tal* beasts, and what she planned to use them for. The answers wouldn't have made a difference, but he was interested. He wanted to know how a quadar like her could afford payment for such a quantity of animals as well as for a party big enough to drive them back. It was a long travel.

"We'll pay you double," Hateri said.

L'rdent's back stiffened, and Taranth was so surprised that all he could do was to grunt his disagreement loudly.

The whelp's primaries were dialed into a focus made sharper by the fact that his hood was pulled back to reveal the skin on his face burned dark from the heats. The curve of his plates rose from his shoulders under the fabric.

Taranth gave the whelp a glare that he wished could burn. "You are here only to observe," he said.

"We need those beasts," Hateri replied.

"That is not how we do it."

Taranth looked at M'ran, who, in return, showed the exact amount of spine Taranth expected of the good council executive—meaning exactly none.

"I do not sell items that are already sold," L'rdent said to Hateri with a tone to his voice that told Taranth the conversation was over.

"Everything has its price," Hateri said. "Name yours and the Families will make it appear."

L'rdent gave a click from the back of his throat that reminded Taranth of a poisonous lizard ready to strike.

"That is enough," Taranth said, rising. "I apologize for taking your time, L'rdent. We will find other ways."

"No," Hateri said firmly.

Taranth's chest constricted.

"We cannot leave here without those beasts," Hateri said, turning to face Taranth. "You know it as well as I do."

Taranth grabbed Hateri by the arm and wrenched him to a standing position. The motion was awkward enough and strong enough that only Hateri's youthful balance kept them from falling over.

"Are your ears as melted as your mind?" Taranth said, spittle splashing as he spoke. "We will not disrespect our host by insinuating his word can be bought out."

Louder noise came from outside.

The door to L'rdent's chamber crashed open, and a volume of yelping voices spilled in. One of the sentries who had met Taranth and the rest of the party put her head into the room.

"Attackers!" she said.

She held a bow in one bony fist, and the sight of quadars scurrying over the beaten ground came from behind her. The light of early Eldoro put the vivid red tinge that was particular to this time of the heat on everything in the background.

Taranth let go of Hateri's arm and stepped to the door.

"Who is it?" L'rdent grabbed a walking staff and struggled to get around the table.

"They carry Festia property," the sentry said.

"Galen," Taranth said, seeing L'rdent's face darken at the same time the answer came to him.

"Call the settlement to their defensive positions," L'rdent said as he shuffled forward.

The sentry blinked her primaries.

"Now!" L'rdent yelled, pounding his staff on the stone floor.

The sentry ran so quickly she left the door gaping open.

"How can I help?" Hateri said.

L'rdent grimaced, then, not responding, stepped out the door to lead the defense.

"We should take cover," M'ran said. "Get to the rest of the group, and drive deeper into the caves until it's over."

Taranth scowled, torn between the need to protect his charges, and the desire to stand with L'rdent and the rest of Harshish Point.

"I'll handle the team," Hateri E'Lar said.

Then he was gone and, without even checking to see if he was out of arrow range, scampered over the open pavilion at the bottom of the depression that served as Harshish Point's central focus.

"The whelp is going to get himself killed," Taranth said.

But inside he was happy as he watched Hateri make it safely through the current of traffic pouring out of the caves, then disappear underground.

M'ran stood with Taranth just outside the door.

Voices were calling, and the cry of *tal* beasts and *neantha* came from the field below and above. Galen had trained *neantha*—if such a thing was possible, anyway. What other depths could she sink to?

"Come on," Taranth said.

He pulled his knife from its sheath along his leg, and ran toward the fray. The blade was all he had, but as a free-ranger he knew he had to take a side—run or fight, either would have its ramifications, and in Taranth's hearts he knew he would never run from L'rdent.

M'ran seemed to be frozen in place as Taranth left the chamber.

Eldoro's heat fell on Taranth's bare head as he crossed out of the shadows. The point rose behind him like a brown tower. The sky was a hazy mass above.

The flat plane of the Harshish Point depression opened out to the west where the ground rose to a ridged lip. After that feature, the terrain forward fell away as if it were a single slab that had just hinged itself downward all at once, leaving cliffs and high ridges that radiated to the northwest and southwest to make a huge funnel that led to the settlement proper. It also meant the natural approach to defending Harshish Point was to take positions on the high ridges and force the opposition to fight uphill. It was why Taranth and the team had come up the pipe, and it was why Galen's party had worked their way up both hills early in the siege.

They wanted the ridges.

The Harshish Point quadars carried whatever weapons they could—knives, swords, and clubs—as they raced forward along those ridges. A few, like the sentry, carried bows, and an even fewer number scurried along carrying handfuls of the explosives that were sometimes used to remove chunks of rock for construction purposes or to clear passages underground. The compounds were dangerous material. Just the sight made him cringe.

Taranth used a series of rocks as shields to get closer to the field.

The wind brought him a whiff of blood. The sound of clashing metal rang out. By the time Taranth came to a position where he could take in the field Galen's party had already made it halfway up the rise.

As he took in the field, two things became clear to him.

This wasn't an even fight. Galen's party far outnumbered the Harshish Point defenders.

And most of her quadars were mounted on *tal* beasts.

Galen didn't need *tal* beasts at all.

Their proposed purchase had been a complete ruse.

Anger filled Taranth as the realization settled.

The end was already clear, and that meant from this point forward everything that happened was just senseless killing.

Just as he pivoted away from a rock, an explosion filled the air with debris and threw Taranth to his knees. When the ground stopped shaking, Taranth struggled to rise, but was pleased he still grasped his knife. A shadow rose over him, and he turned to find a thick-chested *tal* beast rise up before him, the sharp hooves of its front legs churning as it prepared to kick.

Time seemed to stop, then.

The image filled his brain: the animal, raised up on its haunches to three times Taranth's height, its hind feet levered up like an insect's, its broad face looking at the sky as its rider reined it back. All Taranth could see of the quadarti rider was the bottoms of its feet in the skin stirrups and a pants-covered leg bent at the knee.

Then came a noise like none Taranth had ever heard.

A blast—like the explosive, but sharper or crisper—more of a pop or the cracking of a thick bone than a rumble and a shake.

The *tal* beast rider gave a sound like all the air in the sky had left its gut at the same time, and fell away to land in a bloody mess at Taranth's feet.

The beast screamed, but came down without pounding him.

It stood as if unsure what to do next, then it trumpeted and turned away.

Another pop filled the air, this one echoing off the mountainous side of Harshish Point.

Taranth had gathered enough of his wits that he could trace the sound back to the central ridge. There, he saw Hateri standing with his arm extended, pointing a strange device out into the direction of the battle. Pietha stood beside him, carrying a second one of the devices. She handed it to him and took the first from his grasp, then appeared to work some lever as Hateri pointed the new device toward the battlefield again.

Hateri took measure with the thing as if it were a bow. Then another crack came, complete with fire and smoke that spewed from the end of the thing.

Another of the raiding quadars fell.

Hateri waited until Pietha was finished with her work, then they exchanged weapons again. Weapons, Taranth thought, because that's what they were. His memory flashed to when they had come upon the pride of *rela*, and Hateri had grabbed his pack. Taranth assumed he had a large knife inside, but he had been wrong.

The weapon roared again, and another of Galen's raiders grabbed its side, then fell to a knee before being cut down by a Harshish quadar.

Harshish Point defenders roared louder than the explosions then, and louder than the cracks of Hateri's new weapon. Galen's raiders gathered themselves and retreated, slowly at first, but then more rapidly when the weapon cracked again and another of their number fell.

The sound of *tal* beast hooves rumbled in the distance, and a cloud of dust rose up behind them.

Taranth stepped toward the quadar who writhed on the ground at his feet. It was female. A moment ago she had been prepared to cave Taranth's head in with the hoof of her *tal* beast. Now she gasped for air as if unable to take it in. Her primaries blinked, and her central was clamped closed in pain. She clutched at a bloody patch that colored the front of her red and black shirts. They were wet, all six fingers of her hand now blazing with crimson blood as Eldoro's light crossed into the upper sky.

Taranth understood.

Her primary heart had been pierced.

If it had been the second or third, then maybe she would survive, but it was her primary. She was going to die, and her death would be long and painful.

Taranth knelt beside her, raised his knife, and waited.

The quadar swallowed, her throat giving a dry click of resignation. She focused her primaries on Taranth and her central up to Eldoro, took a breath, and then nodded.

"Do it," she whispered through the spaces of her teeth.

Taranth bent down with his knife and performed the only task that could help her.

When he stood up, he was numb.

The quadars of Harshish Point took care of the raiders who had been left behind.

The two living prisoners were staked to the punishment block, where the community would argue over them and assess their fates sometime after Katon rose. The dead were stripped of anything useful, then left facedown on the rock, with arms and legs spread as the old gods had declared was right. Satrak, the Waganat, helped lay them out. Of the expedition's whelps, his blade was the only one bloodstained, his sandals the only ones dirtied with dust from the ridges. When the collective returned to the settlement, the whelp went to the caves while the rest went to drink.

In the distance, the bodies lay in rows.

The desert would take them away before Eldoro came up next.

"Let me see," L'rdent said.

L'rdent and Taranth had arrived at the ridge at the same time and with the same questions: What was the weapon that Hateri E'Lar used, and how did it work?

Hateri raised his device, then handed it to L'rdent.

Pietha held the other in front of her, but did not proffer it.

L'rdent turned the weapon over in his hands.

The device was made of darkened metal, and consisted of a handle similar to the handle of a knife, a middle section as big as Taranth's fist, and a longer barrel from which the fire and smoke had come. Its smell was foul enough it made Taranth's stomachs clench.

"What is it?" Taranth said.

"We call it a gun," Hateri replied. "It was built by our Tegra Family."

"Of the Terilamat?"

"Of course."

Taranth pursed his lips and clicked his throat. "Of course."

"How does it work?" L'rdent said.

Hateri opened his fist to reveal metal pebbles. "These are bullets. The gun shoots them."

"As the bow shoots bolts," L'rdent said, his eyes widening with understanding.

M'ran appeared out of the cave passages and strode through the open pavilion to join them. "What happened?"

"This young quadar saved our lives," L'rdent replied.

Taranth wanted to argue, but he knew better. His hearts were still stuttering over the memory of the *tal* beast ready to strike him.

M'ran's smile was broad and bright. He put his chunky hand on

Hateri's shoulder. "This young quadar can be a little pushy, but he's got his mind right."

L'rdent put the barrel to his nose and sniffed it with the same expression on his face as he had when he inhaled smoke from the burning root. He looked at the bullets in Hateri's hand, and then at the bodies of Galen's raiders that had been carefully arranged in Eldoro's heat.

"I believe we can discuss the *tal* beasts now," L'rdent said, his gaze returning to the weapon. "I'm sure we can find an appropriate price."

Chapter 10

They rested for two more heats, slipping into the caverns to avoid the peak of Eldoro's highpoint.

Taranth watched the whelps.

He saw them speaking. Sharing. Working together in ways they hadn't worked together before and, in fact, in ways he had never seen in the Families before.

The dogmatic clutching of the old ways had always given Taranth a sense of purpose—a sense that what he was holding onto had value of its own sake. A quadar used Eldoro to tell time because that is how you did it, after all. It had always worked for Taranth. Until now, he had been content enough, or at least comfortable enough that he was living life as it was meant to be lived. Until now, he had never truly felt obsolete.

But seeing the whelps working together so freely set him back. Was the intensity of his commitment to the old ways tied more to the price he had paid for his choices than it was to their actual value?

The gun would change everything, he thought, as he watched the young quadars talk with each other that second night. He didn't know *how* it would change everything, but he didn't question that it would. The Tegra Family who made it would rise in stature. Under the council way, that Family would control these weapons. They would decide how much to charge, and who to sell them to.

So, yes, the gun would change everything, including these

young quadars who were gathered with him.

Taranth was certain that no amount of fraternizing they did here would be powerful enough to stop what was coming. He wondered how it would change them. How would they break ties? What pains would they suffer as their people and their clans moved ahead?

Thinking about the future in this way made his head hurt.

Taranth found himself staying above the caves more often than not, preferring to spend time trading stories with L'rdent and the rest of the older, free-range quadars of Harshish Point. Quadars who, like him, lived in a desert that was constantly prepared to kill them, because, when it was all tallied, they didn't belong anywhere else.

They laughed about the heats in the way only a desert quadar can. They swapped stories about how the lack of water could make your central read pure black. They exchanged tales about the raw terror an outsider feels when they hear the sounds of a *neantha* pack on the hunt in the middle of the darkest nights of Absolute Convergence. They commiserated with a lone quadar who lost his water, and discussed the way the coarse grit of sulfur turns into the burning water when the infrequent rain actually fell all the way to the desert rock in the wrong places.

They asked him questions, too.

"Who are the whelps?"

"What is that gun?"

"Must be a cluster mess to get a dozen of them here alive."

They were interested in the whelps in ways that justified Taranth's own sense of confusion. He explained how the young ones spoke differently. Dressed differently. Thought differently. He did his best to pretend he understood what the gun did, but found it really didn't matter. The quadars here treated him as if he was the expert when it came to all things whelp, and not a one of them could counter his viewpoints. It was, he thought, an odd thing to have a sense of expertise about.

He wondered if this was what it was like to be a philosopher or a priest.

They argued about L'rdent, though, and what it meant that he would now have one of these weapons.

Taranth had visited Harshish Point before, but this was the first time he had let himself be a true part of the gathering. He was surprised to find that sitting with these free-rangers made him feel like he had a home. Not a really a place, but an unusual sense of fitting into something. A sense of belonging. For the first time since Alena died, he almost did not feel like he was strange.

He wondered if this might be his last expedition, or if he might come back. And if he did come back, was he getting old enough that he might decide to just stay here forever?

Taranth watched the weather, too, trying to judge if the squalls that had delayed their way in had been random storms, or whether they were the first calls of a burning wind—one of the massive storms that made the time of Convergence so dangerous, but were rare with the heats so far apart.

His reputation was at stake.

The whelplings had followed him because they'd been told to, but now they had seen Hateri's insolence, and they had seen him win. They were spending the heats with Hateri, listening to his guidance. M'ran was almost certainly right in his prediction of Hateri's future as a power broker. Watching it happen made Taranth feel older still.

"The pup's going to take your team," one of the *katja* harvesters told him while they were playing a game of dice. She was a free-ranger, but not quite as old as Taranth. Something past two full cycles rather than three.

"He can have it," Taranth said, rolling and losing at the same time.

The quadar laughed and pounded him on the arm so hard it hurt. "Responsibility is overrated, eh, my friend."

The answer annoyed him.

Like everyone here, she was a quadar who wanted independence.

She seemed reliable enough in the way she lived her life—a quadar who would do her part for the whole, but who he suspected was more pragmatic than principled. To live a life in the desert and *not* do the things one needs to do is to have the desert take you young. So she went to the *katja* sheets every other heat, and she brought in her allotment of the root that sustained much of life here. She went out on the hunts when needed, and she stabled animals when shamed into it. But her presence here was not otherwise of much note. She was baked thin, and her eyes were shot through with a network of veins that came from overindulging in a certain mold that grew in the caves. She lived as free of the Families and the council as he did, but he disdained her lack of interest in anything else and especially her lack of interest in *movement*.

He did not want to settle in a place and then have nothing to look forward to but a walk to the *katja* sheets and a night's worth of oblivion.

And yet, watching Hateri and the rest of the whelps as they went about their own preparations reminded him of the limits of his time.

That before long what he wanted or what he did not want might not matter.

Watching the whelps left him keenly aware that he would not live forever.

Chapter 11

As their fourth heat at Harshish Point passed, Taranth and M'ran selected three healthy *tal* beasts that had been freshly watered, and arranged for three flatbed carts with axels that were still straight and that, though weathered, were still sturdy and firm. They acquired water, hard nuts, bags of *katja* bread, and dried meat. They gathered rope and extra bags, and coverings they would need for the salvaging.

The whelplings loaded these onto the carts for the return trip.

The rest, and now the activity, raised the entire group's spirits. The group was fresher now, and clearly feeling stronger.

Yanil's knee had healed, and their time down in the cool caves had given everyone's bruises the chance to fade. Their desert-addled minds had gathered back together. They were a grizzled crew, now. Or at least it seemed that way to the whelps. Their success in arriving here meant they were experienced desert dwellers, and Hateri's use of the guns had raised all of their statures.

The whelps also recognized the value of the *tal* beasts.

These muscular, six-legged animals with fine, bristly pelts smelled horrendous, but were otherwise perfectly formed for the desert—loping with smooth gaits that seemed to take no energy, and when properly managed, able to travel for many heats without water. Their shoulders came to Taranth's chin, and their heads rose taller. Pulling the carts, even heavily loaded, would not be an issue for them. Knowing that the carts were full of supplies raised spirits even further.

The expedition ate together that last night at Harshish Point, and they listened to Cestral give a concert on the mouth harp she had found in the stores under the rock. Some told stories. Others sang.

In the noise of the evening, Taranth almost missed the moment where Pietha whispered something into Hateri's ear and slipped a gift into his hand. It was a small thing. Not something he could make out in the thin light of the cave, which was probably for the best. He felt voyeur enough just seeing what he had seen.

When Hateri slipped away with Pietha once again, Taranth felt blood stir through all three of his hearts, but was happy to find that it did not make him angry.

The next morning, though Eldoro had not yet risen, all of the team was ready. This fact pleased Taranth beyond reason.

They chewed roots and drank water, then loaded themselves into the back of the carts and began their return journey to the mesa where they hoped the Taranth Stone still lay.

Taranth guided the lead cart, and the group selected Hateri and Yip to guide the other two—at least to start out.

The trip began with a lurch as each animal moved forward to make their way through the slot leading out of the settlement. Wheels ground against sand-lined rock, and the light of Eldoro cast its redness across the ground. The axles squeaked behind the footfalls of the animals, and the stench of the beasts filled Taranth's senses. The wooden platform beneath his feet bounced to the rhythm of the *tal* beast's stride.

"You could never know this was a battlefield just a few heats back," M'ran said as he held onto the rail to keep from pitching over.

Taranth clicked the back of his throat. M'ran was right. The desert had already smoothed over the events that had transpired there only three heats back. He recalled the sensation of plunging his knife blade into the dying raider, the pressure of the blade against his hand and the firmness of the stroke as he completed the slice. A detachment came over him as he remembered watching the quadar's blood soak back into the sand.

"The desert reclaims what it needs," he said.

"You're a fatalistic nob, aren't you?"

"Just telling the truth."

"Then let's hope the desert doesn't need your Taranth Stone."

Taranth snarfed. "That would be the grand irony, wouldn't it? The council sends their whelplings to gather the Light That Falls from the Sky only to have the desert beat them to it?"

"We've already beaten the desert to it, my friend. Now we're just trying to keep it from stealing what is already ours."

Taranth turned his central toward M'ran.

An entire stream of thoughts ran through his mind, but he said none of them. The desert had nothing but time, and in the end would always win. It wasn't Taranth's job to teach him that. Instead, he turned back to the *tal* beast and let the rawhide reins go looser in his hands.

The animal picked up the pace, heading westward and gently south, back to the place where the Taranth Stone should be waiting for them.

M'ran continued to give small talk, but Taranth was too busy watching the carts to pay him much mind.

Hateri stood tall at the front of the cart to Taranth's left, reins of the *tal* beast in one hand. His jaw jutted forward into the wind. The hood of his field robe billowed behind him in the desert breeze. He was, Taranth admitted, the picture of leadership. Bold, direct, and strong.

Taranth sighed.

Young.

Taranth himself had been like that once, but that was a long time ago.

Though no one else complained, the weather remained almost too clear and too calm for Taranth's liking. It gave the heats a sameness that numbed his mind. Eldoro rising, *piela* and *kax* scurrying in the dry dust, *jah* overhead. Those were the same every heat.

A herd of fleet-footed *razo* broke up the monotony of the third morning. As the *razo* gathered around a root bramble and filled themselves, Taranth took the moment to point out how two *razo* played sentry against any *rela* pride or a *neantha* pack that might come while the rest ate, and how the sentries were left the choicest vines in return. When the *razo* were gone, he took the party to the grazing fields and showed the younger quadars how the animals had eaten only the leaves, leaving the roots themselves intact so that the sheet would yield another such breakfast later.

"They're like the *katja* harvesters in Harshish Point," said Yip.

Taranth smiled, and they moved on.

With the team's renewed confidence and the *tal* beasts providing steady progress, the company made it back to the mesa in only five heats' travel.

The whelplings took much of one heat to load the scattered components of the Taranth Stone onto the carts.

Most pieces could be handled by one quadar alone, while others needed a pair. The largest section, however, required eight of them to lift, and then they could barely balance it on the cart.

They secured the larger pieces with thick-twined ropes, and wrapped up smaller pieces in sacks and boxes that they affixed firmly to the rails.

"We've seen the winds," Hateri said when Ogala had carelessly left a sack open to the air. He leveraged himself up onto the cart and tied off the sack, then ensured it was strapped snug to the side rail. "They need to be tight," he said as he hopped down.

He gave Ogala a nod, which she returned.

From that point on, the work was done well.

The load took less time to gather than Taranth expected.

The gathering stood dirty from their work, but strong and proud under the fading smear of Eldoro in the clouds.

"I think we've got everything," Hateri finally said. "Should we leave?"

They looked to Taranth for confirmation.

"There is more heat left," Taranth said to Hateri, "but we've worked hard. I think it best we camp, don't you?"

Hateri hesitated, then apparently realized he had just been asked for advice. He scanned the sky, taking in the positions of Eldoro and Katon, who was now rising noticeably earlier each heat in her quest to catch her brother.

"Yes," he said. "I think you're right. It would be good to rest. Use the lee of the mesa for camp. Everyone drink what they can."

"Then let's do that," Taranth said.

The gathering broke. They relaxed and watched as Eldoro sank to the west.

Taranth gathered with them and pointed out exactly how far Katon had already slipped up on her brother.

"See how she is nearing half her highpoint now," he said, pointing Katon's light out against the sky above as the last of Eldoro was fading.

Yip added, "When we started she was just arriving on the far side when Eldoro was leaving the sky."

"Yes," Taranth said.

He took a large stone, then, and he used the edge of his knife to mark the shapes of the shadows that Katon and Eldoro gave to the ground. He spoke of their mixed patterns, how the shadow pattern alone could let them tell what part of the year it was, and in fact what part of the cycle they were in.

The gathering listened.

They asked questions, and Taranth was amazed to see the lessons take hold, and how they began to teach each other. All quadars were taught the basic paths of the heats, of course. They were impossible to miss. But the art of shadow reading was a different thing all together.

"Can you tell us the patterns?" Satrak Waganat asked.

A depth lay in his gaze that Taranth understood better than any other. It was the first thing the whelp had said to Taranth the entire trip.

"I can tell you them, yes. But to truly know them requires you to watch them carefully for entire cycles."

"Show me," the Waganat said.

So Taranth did.

Later, when Eldoro was hard set and Katon was past her highpoint, Taranth went to sit beside Hateri.

The quadar made no movement to indicate Taranth existed, though Taranth knew Hateri was aware of him, as were the rest of the gathering.

Hateri was finishing his meal, chewing quietly on dried *piela* lizard and sipping from water. He had just finished arranging the night water catch.

"You will lead the team home," Taranth said, speaking loudly enough to be heard across the distance but in a voice controlled enough to ensure the rest of the party heard it as a simple statement of fact rather than sense any implied threat.

He clicked his throat to show he was done.

Hateri's primaries glanced his way. "Trying to save your skin?" he whispered.

"Do you think it needs saving?"

"This is your expedition, Elder," he said in a stronger voice.

Taranth raised the ridge over his central and looked at the rest of the party, seeing something that he took as surprise on M'ran's face.

"The young replace the old," he said. "It is the quadarti way. It's the way of the desert, too. I brought us to the stone. You've earned the right to lead us back."

Hateri stopped chewing and just looked at Taranth.

Taranth smiled in the coolness of the evening. He stood and, while the rest of the party watched, went to his bedding and slipped into the dust cover. Pausing, he pointed to the timer box that was still hanging from Hateri's belt. "What time do we leave?"

A self-conscious expression spread over Hateri's face.

He looked at the device, then to Taranth. His central scanned the sky where a pair of *jah* were out hunting.

"We'll leave when Eldoro crests," he said.

The team seemed to smile as one.

Taranth used his central to scan the late sky, then lay back on his blanket. The roof of his lean-to groaned in the wind.

"Don't forget to set the guard watch," he said.

Perhaps this next generation of quadars would turn out all right after all, he thought as he closed his eyes.

Then he slipped off to a deep sleep.

Chapter 12

The burning wind came three heats later.

It came suddenly, and ferociously.

It came just as the team had cleared the craggy series of obsidian crevasses Taranth's da had called Death's Teeth, a line of jagged rock that could have broken the force of the gale if the group had been just that much slower.

Instead, the storm caught the team on the long run of flat land between Death's Teeth and the eastern ring of outer Esgarat.

Until then, the weather had been clear.

Almost no wind.

Eldoro had been an orange blot high overhead, the sky a yellowed dome of clouds that seemed to stretch into forever.

The storm started with one gust, a simple duster that spiraled upward and disappeared quickly.

If Taranth had been paying attention, he would have stopped them then. If he had been sharp, he would have had them bind the carts for shelter and lay the *tal* beasts down against the wind to give them protection. But he was striding along at the back of the team, stretching his legs and worrying only about their direction while Hateri led them forward.

By the time he noticed the wall of sand rising up, it was too late.

The wind came like the blow of a hammer.

The heat like the blasting of a furnace.

The sand like the swirling of razors.

Visibility was gone in seconds.

Taranth shouted orders, fell to his knees, and wrapped his hood over his face, hoping the others remembered their lessons.

The youngest of the *tal* beasts gave its piercing call of danger as it broke from the line. The cart behind the *tal* twisted and turned with its movement, then caught the wind and the inertia of its sudden change in direction raised it up. The cart tilted and rolled, contents and quadars falling to the ground. The animal panicked and tried to run, its form a dark shadow fading into the orange depths.

The wind was already so strong Taranth could not hear the party scream.

The sand-darkened shape of Yip Kil was standing up ahead, then she was gone. He crawled toward the others, keeping low to the ground to give the storm less area to grab, keeping his fingers wide to give him full purchase. The strength of the wind made it like climbing a sheer cliff sideways. Sand burned anything that was exposed.

He kept his eyes mostly shut, squinting ahead.

A dark lump lay before him.

It was M'ran.

"Did you see anyone else?" he yelled into his friend's ears, but the question was answered for itself when M'ran turned to face him. M'ran's eyes, central and both primaries, were squeezed tightly shut and both hands were over them. He was groaning and grunting, "Burns!" He screamed when Taranth grabbed him. When he heard Taranth's voice the screams turned to pleading. "Make it stop!" he called. "Make it stop!" But Taranth knew that wasn't going to happen anytime soon, and while the pain would subside M'ran's sight was likely gone forever.

"Stay here!" he commanded. "Keep down!"

The wind battered him as he pulled himself forward.

A trick of the current picked him up and skittered him along the ground like so much dry brush. Skin tore from his fingers and knees as he tried to catch himself. For an instant he thought he was dead, but luck was his. The wind deposited him painfully into a thicket whose thorns pierced his skin and whose dry wood chattered like bone music in the angry swirl. His arm was battered, but he caught a hold that let him keep steady and gather himself back up.

He pulled himself out of the bush.

Using his bruised arm as a shield, he peered through the curtain of sand.

He had no idea which direction he had come from.

So he did the only thing a quadar of the desert knows to do.

He hugged the ground close, and he waited for the storm to subside.

When it was over, Taranth went back toward the team's last location.

His legs and back burned from where thorns had impaled him. He would have to dig them out later, a painful process that he wasn't looking forward to, but one that was far better than to leave them to fester. His neck and arm hurt, but would heal. The wind still gusted but it was a calmer beast now, settling to simply beat the folds of his robes against his chest, scrub his skin, and carry dust away.

The landscape was desolate, open, and barren.

He saw no one, not even a blind M'ran.

A cart had been overturned nearby, looking more like a cage than a form of transportation now. The largest pieces of the Taranth Stone remained lashed to it, trapped inside. As he drew near, a mound of sand stirred and a *tal* beast rose up, still attached to the cart. The animal gave a plaintive call, and an awkward shake that scattered clouds of dust. Taranth grunted his admiration. It was a grizzled thing, this *tal* beast, but it knew how to turn its back to the wind and let the sand build its protection.

He ran his hand over the animal's shoulder as he released it from the cart, leaving it free to move, knowing the *tal* beast understood the idea of safety in numbers and that it would stay nearby.

He found three bodies—Cestral of the Taler Family, Ogala of the Tael, and Gis'le of the Ombat—obviously trampled by the rampaging *tal*, their exposed faces sandblasted and raw. Supplies were scattered across the plain, as were a few smaller pieces of the Taranth Stone. The wreckage of a second cart was a hundred paces away. He could not readily see the third, but it had been lighter than the others because it had carried supplies rather than pieces of the salvage.

Hidden inside the folds of the wind, he heard the sound of sobbing.

He limped to a large boulder and found Hateri sitting against the rock, desolate, head thrown back, and facing the direct heat of Eldoro as trails of tears crisscrossed his dust-caked face. The young quadar appeared unhurt beyond the simple bumping or bruising that was unavoidable in a burning wind.

Taranth stopped before him, his shadow putting Hateri into darkness.

"I killed them," Hateri said when he opened his primaries.

"No," Taranth said. He sat down beside Hateri. "If any of us killed them, it was me. I should have been paying more attention."

This was the truth, and he knew it. Taranth had grown lazy. He had let the desert bait him. And he had given himself to the fates in another way, too. He should have known better than to become close to the whelps. The desert takes what it wants, and for Taranth the desert had always wanted it all.

They sat for a while until Taranth spoke again.

"This kind of thought is useless, though. In the desert we take care of ourselves."

"I can't accept that."

"It's the way of the quadarti." Taranth said. "Come, perhaps we can find others." He proffered his hand, and the council member's son took it. Hateri's eyes were glassy and his expression seemed etched in stone, but he went with Taranth and together they searched the fields of dust.

They found Yip Kil had been tumbled to death.

M'ran was dead from a large piece of broken lumber driven through his chest at a vicious angle.

A second *tal* beast survived intact, lifting itself from the ground and shaking sand from its pale mane. Its cart was nearby, still workable with some fixing of one wheel.

Of the others, they found no sign.

They made camp and gathered what pieces of the Taranth Stone they could, loading them all onto the two carts that remained, lucky that the largest piece had remained lashed to the most stable of them.

Hateri turned to the bodies, then, coming to Gis'le first.

"What are you doing?" Taranth said.

"Bringing her back," the young quadar replied.

Taranth shook his head.

"We have to bring them back," Hateri said.

"The trip is too long," he replied. "The stench of flesh will bring the *rela* and the *neantha* or any one of a hundred scavengers."

They argued long and hard.

Hateri cried.

Taranth stood firm, though it nearly broke him to see the whelp's anger. "The desert will claim them either way," he said. "Better for all if they are left to feed the land this way."

When they woke the following heat, the two of them silently loaded everything they had onto the two remaining carts, and yoked those carts onto the two remaining *tal* beasts.

Then, together, they made their way toward the One Great Esgarat, and toward the council.

Just the two of them.

Chapter 13

They subsisted on almost nothing for five hands of heats. Only a single water catch between them. They huddled with the *tal* beasts to wait out another of the burning winds. To eat, they had only a few salvaged bags of *katja* bread and what roots and meats they had found in the wreckage. It was survival the old way, but it was survival.

They took turns driving the beasts, following paths and crevasses that lined the outer plains until they found the only pass in the mountains that would let the carts through. It was also a pass patrolled by the *neantha*, a pack of which took one of the *tal* beasts their first evening there. Both of the quadars had faded to lucid sleep, and the pack came in unfettered. Not that it would have mattered. The *neantha* singles out the weak first, and that *tal* beast had been laboring. Taranth and Hateri had already begun to plan how to proceed with just one beast and one cart.

The pass gave shade, and sometimes liquid would pool in cracks in the rock where they could siphon off enough of a splash to almost fill their mouths, which had been enough, barely, to traverse the pass and enter the Esgarat, to push the *tal* harder across the inner plain, and finally to arrive at Esgarat City. Together, they had traveled across the desolation of the desert with the *tal* beast and the cart. Together, they had made it.

This alone was why Taranth thought the young quadar would survive.

He had made it this far. The desert did not seem to want him yet.

Taranth stood at the door of Jafred E'Lar's private chambers.

The time was late, and Katon was near her setting point, yet there was still some time before Eldoro would appear to the east. Divergence was drawing to its end. The darkness of this time of the year was not complete, but was still enough that his central gave him the bulk of his sight. Now that the racket of the *tal* beast and the cart's creaking wheels were finished, the street around him was silent. The coolness of Esgarat City settled over him.

He wore only a ragged cloth around his waist now. Dry rotting sandals wrapped around his ankles. They were old and ripped. He had repaired them six hundred times—or was it six million? His skin peeled. His head ached. His body no longer felt like it was his own.

He did not want to know how he smelled.

The door swung open.

A servant stood there, his robe hastily thrown on and his eyes still clouded with sleep.

"I have come to see the council member," Taranth said.

"It is late," the servant replied, scanning Taranth with clear suspicion. "The council member is sleeping."

"He will want to speak with me."

The quadar looked at him.

Their one remaining animal and its cart stood behind Taranth, dusty in the distance, nibbling the tender grasses that grew under a well-pruned *grisa* tree. The cart, loaded down now with the entire remains of the Taranth Stone, was still lashed to its harness. Hateri, also sprawled in the back and hopefully still asleep, could not be seen. The animal was past the point of exhaustion, as was Taranth. The young E'Lar would probably survive. He was breathing, anyway, though he had nothing left.

Taranth's bones ached as he stood before this servant. His head pounded. He wanted only for this job to be finished.

"I can see if he has an appointment tomorrow," the servant said, beginning to close the door.

"What is your name?" Taranth replied.

"Pana."

"Well, Pana," Taranth said, making his voice as sharp as he could. "If you put me off until tomorrow, I will tell council member E'Lar it was your doing that he was unable to see his son for an extra heat. Given the state he's in, I hope you are prepared to pay that price."

Pana hesitated, but Taranth could tell his resolve had already crumbled.

"Wait in the garden, please," the servant said.

Taranth sat on a bench in the silent and still air while he waited for the servant to wake the council member. The sensation of nothingness was familiar to him now. He felt like he wasn't there, like he wasn't even inside his own skin. When he listened closely enough, however, he realized he wasn't alone at all. Wind whipped over buildings and brought a soft clatter from the lines strung with drying cloth hanging free. Strange noises like that. Noises you don't hear on the desert plains. Noises you don't hear in the core of the caves.

The bench was made of cast metals.

Its edges pressed into the bony ridge of his spine. The surface felt odd to him, too, smooth and soft despite their edges, painted with a thick coat of white. The stones that covered the path below his torn sandals were soft and pebbled. The aroma of flower buds, open for the evening air, gave the garden a scent that Taranth found to be too sweet. The idea that quadars lived like this was hard for him to grasp.

The scratch of a lizard rushing over the pebbles came as Jafred E'Lar raced across the manor yard, the tails of his robe flying free behind him, and two other servants just behind the tails.

"Where is my son?"

Taranth levered himself to stand up, then nodded to where the *tal* beast and its cart stood.

"In the back."

"Thank the old gods," Jafred replied. "Where is the rest of the team?"

"Dead."

Jafred's face paled.

"All but your son," Taranth added.

The council member ground his teeth, but was already rushing to the cart.

By the time Jafred slumped onto a bench across the path from him, darkness was at its depth. The council servers had brought Taranth water and food—baked bread with *havra* and fresh hard nuts. Despite his hunger, Taranth ate sparely, knowing his stomachs were not ready yet. He drank the water though, emptying several decanters.

"He will make it?" Taranth said after Jafred appeared, concern etching his face.

The council member nodded. "He needs water, food, and rest. But he should heal."

"His body, anyway," Taranth said.

"Yes, his body, anyway."

"I have completed your assignment," Taranth said.

"Tell me about it."

Taranth wrapped his six fingers over his knees and used his central to stare into the darkness.

In a quiet voice, he told Jafred about his son's work.

"His team loved him," Taranth said at the end of the story. "They would have torn down the Esgarat Mountains if he had asked them to. If he can overcome this moment, he will make a difference."

"Thank you," Jafred said.

Taranth understood the conflict he saw in the council member's primaries. In the morning, Jafred would have to tell his fellow council members that their sons and daughters had died while his own survived.

"What is that?" Jafred said, glancing at the cart as if he had just noticed it now, a restraint that impressed Taranth.

"The Light That Fell from the Sky. What is left of it, anyway."

The council member went to examine it.

Taranth followed him, already feeling better for the new liquid in his body.

Jafred's eyes grew wide with wonder as he took in the salvage.

His hearts pounded as he put his hand on the sandblasted surface. His skin tingled in the near-damp air of Katon falling. Even in the darkness, Jafred could see strange boxes inside the shell, boxes filled with equipment and wires and other pieces that thrilled him and scared him at the same time. The burnt places on the outer shell of the biggest piece reminded him that the light was said to blaze like fire in the sky.

After all this time, those stories had actually given him to wonder about gods, both old and new, but the equipment laid out before him now spoke only of engineers and inventors.

He flashed on Taranth's story of Hateri and the guns.

The guns hadn't surprised him. Nothing the Families did would surprise him.

This device, however…

Jafred had already seen enough of it to know that no quadar of any Family could have done the work it took to make it.

The Light That Fell from the Sky had come from someplace else.

This was the moment, he would tell his son later, that the world felt somehow bigger, this moment when it felt to him that something important was waiting for them, something bigger than any quadar, be they scholar, philosopher, council member, or priest, could ever know.

This was the moment, also, when he understood that the Light That Fell From the Sky had to remain a council secret.

The device could not be given to any single Family. That much was obvious. And to discuss it publicly would be to set the Families onto a squabble that would result, eventually, in the find being cut up into small segments that each could exploit to their strengths.

That was the quadarti way—or at least it had been in the past.

Jafred took a long time to examine the full nature of the find.

Upward, backward, he bent and stooped to examine each piece with intensity.

The device was remarkable.

Finally, however, Jafred's curiosity was sated.

He turned to tell Taranth that his payment would be delivered at the time when Eldoro rose. He turned to say that he wanted Taranth to stay in his quarters for this night and for as many nights as he would—because this was perhaps the most incredible thing he had ever seen, and because Jafred wanted Taranth to brief him about everything that happened, where exactly it had been found, how exactly the storm had come, what exactly they had left behind.

But when he turned to tell Taranth these things, he found himself alone.

The guide had left the garden.

Honoring the Fallen

Chapter 14

Hateri woke to the smell of boiled *havra* and spiced tea.

His first thought was that he was dreaming, but the breeze came through his second-floor room like it had always done before the expedition, and he recognized his closets and the study desk still covered with the assignments he had left undone prior to leaving. Those assignments seemed trivial now. Stupid. Who cared which Family owned the making of draperies or which constructed building foundations?

His second thought was that everything about him hurt with a version of pain that began with deep stabbing in his chest and ended with a scour that burned over his cracked lips. The skin around his forehead was stretched thin and too small for his head. A memory of gouging his leg came to him. But none of these could compete with the pain that struck when he thought about Pietha and the others.

He was wearing sleepskins.

Another moment of absurdity. One minute he was in foul-smelling rags and falling to the ground, the next he was here, in these sleepskins.

Then, for a moment, Hateri panicked, searching the room until he saw his belts and their pouches hung over the back of the chair in the far corner.

"You're awake."

Chanzi, the council member's cook, placed a tray filled with bowls, plates, and a cup of tea on the stand next to Hateri's bed. The aroma of *havra* became suddenly stronger. A napkin sat at the tray's edge, folded properly.

It all seemed so absolutely surreal.

"I'll call your father."

"Where is Taranth?" he said, his voice still thick with sleep. He drew a deep breath and winced as his ribs burned. Moving hurt.

Chanzi wagged a finger in his direction. "Don't go trying to get me into trouble. You know I'll be leaving the answering to your father." Chanzi helped him sit up in the bed, and put the tray near him. Then he left to ring the council member.

Hateri's stomachs throbbed with the anticipation of food. When he brought the spoon to his lips, the spicy sting of *havra* soup against his lips nearly made him weep. His skin was stretched across his cheekbones, and it hurt to twist his face into any expression. He wondered what he looked like. Probably not good.

After three spoons, he sat back to rest.

He wanted to drink the tea, but the idea of more hot liquid on his lips made him cringe. He drank water instead, finishing all of it, though at first he used the smaller sips he had learned to take in the desert.

Footsteps pounded in the corridor outside.

"Hateri!" his father's voice came just as he stepped into the room. "How do you feel?"

"Sore."

"The medics say you should stay in bed for several heats, and it could be several hands of heats before everything comes back. You are a pretty sick quadar."

"Where is Taranth?"

His father pulled a seat forward and sat down beside the crèche. "He left."

Pursing his lips sent a flare of pain across Hateri's face. He couldn't imagine Taranth staying in Esgarat City, but to not have him here felt wrong.

Hateri closed all three eyes.

The last heats of the trip were still a blur, but the rest was coming back.

Every step had been filled with pain, but Taranth prodded him, kept him going by goading him and pushing him. He kept Hateri talking about Pietha by telling him about Alena, a female Taranth himself had once loved. Taranth forced him to eat, made him drink. He was pretty sure Taranth loaded him onto the back of the cart at one point, but he couldn't be certain. All he remembered for sure was coming to consciousness with the flat boards of the cart jostling below him and the hard surface of the Taranth Stone pressing him up against the rails.

These were tough, painful memories. But they were easier to deal with than the images of his friends lying facedown, arms outstretched in the sand, waiting for the desert to reclaim them as he pulled away.

"Are you all right, son?"

"How could he do that?"

"Do what?"

"How could Taranth leave?"

His father sighed, and shrugged. "What can I say? He's of the desert. He didn't even take his payment."

Hateri sighed against pain. Taranth was gone. The idea suddenly hurt him more than anything else.

"Tell me about your trip."

"He didn't even stay to tell you what happened?"

"He told me what happened."

Hateri sat back. At least there was that. "Then I don't want to talk about it."

"You're going to have to talk about it sometime, Hateri. If nothing else, the Families will want to hear it from you."

"Not now."

"All right. But we do need to talk about the Light That Fell from the Sky."

Hateri grinned. "The Taranth Stone," he said.

"The Taranth Stone?" Jafred said.

"That's what we named the Light That Fell from the Sky."

"Because?"

Hateri swallowed and clicked his throat to indicate he was thinking. "It's a bit of a story," he said, deciding he didn't want to talk about it. "You've seen the stone?"

"I've had it put into a safe place for now."

"Where?"

His father glanced to the door, then out the window. They were small movements, but clear to Hateri.

"I need you to agree to help me," Jafred said. "The Families are going to want to hear from you, and it is crucial that you tell them that the expedition found nothing."

"What?"

"You came up empty. There was nothing there to find."

"That doesn't make any sense. If you've seen it, you know it's important. If we pretend it never existed, it makes all the sacrifice mean nothing."

His father bent close. "I agree completely. We need to study it. But it is precisely because I've seen it and precisely because we need to study it that I'm telling you we have to hide its existence."

"I can't believe I'm hearing this."

Hateri clenched all three eyes, then opened them again.

His father was perched on the edge of his seat and leaned forward, his entire body engaged in this discussion.

"You know how much I believe in bringing the Families together, Hateri."

"I used to."

"But you haven't seen them as I've seen them. They aren't ready for this kind of step right now, especially after losing their namesakes. We need to give them time. If the Families see this thing, they will tear it apart. They will take their stakes and make of them what they will. And if we tear this system apart, we'll never be able to discover what it was to begin with."

"I don't know," Hateri said, his brain still fogged.

"Yes, you do."

Hateri remembered his compatriots. The way they worked together. He remembered Pietha. "You didn't see us," he said. "We were a team. We made it work. The Families can agree to keep the Taranth Stone in one piece."

"Don't be ignorant. It won't happen that way."

"They died for this, Father. My friends. They died doing what I said, and now you want me to hide the very thing they died for? What kind of a quadar do you think I am?"

"I think you're the kind of quadar who can see what is right for the whole of our civilization."

Hateri clenched his jaw.

His father spoke. "I need you to tell the Families that you did not find the Light."

"I can't do that."

They sat together for several moments while breeze from the window filled the room. Sounds filtered up from below, distant voices echoed, and the hustle of quadars going about their lives seemed to come from everywhere at once.

Hateri's father stood, then straightened his shirts.

"You need to rest," he said. "We'll discuss it later."

Then he left to do whatever it was that a council member did—a set of tasks that Hateri now had no interest in whatsoever.

He grimaced as he reached for the bowl.

The soup was cold.

CHAPTER 15

When Jafred E'Lar left his son's bedside, he strode purposefully through the manor and toward the gates that led to his carriages. He was late to his chamber, which meant he would be late to the discussion of the Tael Family's request to alter their permissions to farm roots. Not that any of that mattered to him right then.

He supposed he should be proud of his son, but he had no time for such luxury.

The Families would hear of Hateri's return. They would want information, and they would want that information now. Hateri had to be made to understand this. If the council was found to be withholding such news, the Families would be completely within their rights to remove Jafred and the rest of the elders from their positions. Yet, he couldn't let the Families strip the Light That Fell from the Sky, this "Taranth Stone," as Hateri called it—which is exactly what they would do if they got their hands on it. The council needed to understand exactly what this was before letting anyone else know about it.

"Council Member Jafred?" Pana said from the doorway behind.

Despite the early hour and the long night before, Pana was dressed properly as he stood in the doorway.

"What is it?" Jafred said.

"You have visitors in the receiving room."

Jafred dropped his chin to his chest, using his central to check that Eldoro's heat had barely risen. That was even faster than he expected.

"Who are they?"

"Representatives of the Waganat and Ombat Families."

Steeling himself, he walked back to his dwelling.

"Please have a message sent to the council that I will be running late," he told Pana as he walked past.

His visitors were not just representatives of the Families.

One was Musef Ombat, the other Ranya Waganat.

The Family heads.

They sat stoically on two of the four ornamental guest stools in the room, having taken positions as far from each other as the small chamber would allow. The Ombat leader wore formal leggings and a thick tunic made of root fabric. His boots had been shined with fresh oils recently enough that they showed no dust. The Waganat wore his Family crest on a ring that encircled his head above the central, and a loose robe that pooled to the floor. Both Families were of the Terilamat clan.

Jafred understood the game.

As a council member from that same clan, Jafred would be expected to provide them information before the others.

"I am so pleased to see you both," Jafred said as he sat between them. "I assume you are here due to news of my son's return."

"We understand he returned alone," Ranya Waganat said.

Jafred drew a deep breath.

"There is no good way to say this, Ranya, but it is my sad duty to tell you that all of the party was lost with the exception of my son."

Though it had probably been expected, the news settled harshly on both quadars.

"M'ran?" Musef Ombat replied as he unfolded his hands, and folded them again. "And the guide?"

"Only the guide returned with my son, but he left before I could even have him paid."

"That is unfortunate."

Jafred made an agreeing motion. "I am sorry for the news."

"But you still have your son," said the Ombat.

"I apologize for my good fortune amid the tragedy."

"Do we know what happened?"

"Yes, we do. The guide described the horrible events of a burning storm."

Jafred didn't have to put on an act for his shudder to show revulsion. The idea of living through a burning wind was terrifying. But the moment gave him a thought. If he could sell this properly, perhaps he could spare the need to have Hateri speak publicly at all.

"I am sure there is more to learn," Jafred said. "And as I learn more I will gladly share it all. But Hateri is quite ill. He's desert dry and has suffered a contusion to his leg. His memory is also somewhat clouded by his baking and the dire nature of his travels. The medical staff has told me it could be many heats before he is prepared to speak on the subject with any clarity."

"I see," Musef replied.

"Do we know what they found?" the Waganat said.

Jafred measured a careful sigh, thinking of his philosopher's background and the debates and discussions he had held in the past. He believed every such conversation has this particular moment to it—the time where the path of the present diverges into multiple futures. These were dangerous moments, yes, but they were also thrilling.

Options collapse at these points.

Choices must be made.

Ranya Waganat was the least sentimental of the Family heads. Young Satrak Waganat was his nephew a few times over, and as such, the loss was real. But Ranya Waganat was a developer of technologies and an arranger of businesses above all other things. His Family was intertwined with more projects than any other Family Jafred knew, and he knew them all. Ranya was the quadar Jafred feared the most when it came to the Light That Fell from the Sky.

He kept his gaze impassive as he focused all three eyes on the Waganat.

"The search team found nothing," Jafred said. "Taranth—the plainsguide—brought Hateri home on cart pulled by a half-dead *tal* beast, but the rest of the cart was empty."

His visitors absorbed his comment.

"Perhaps," Jafred continued, "that is why the plainsguide disappeared without word and without payment."

"Perhaps we will find the plainsguide and find out," Waganat replied.

"I have already dispatched a team," Jafred said, knowing now he would need to do this before he left for his office.

"We should each charter our own search teams," Ombat said.

"Yes," Waganat added. "Two or three efforts are better than one."

"Indeed," Jafred said, knowing he could not forestall them. "The more eyes on a subject the better."

The Waganat clicked agreement from deep in his throat.

"We will want to hear your son speak when he is strong enough to handle such a task."

"Rest assured I will call all the affected Families together as soon as it's possible."

"Terilamat first," Musef said.

"Of course," Jafred said. "Always."

Chapter 16

With the painkilling aid of mashed *chi* leaf, the new sensation of having had enough water, and the comfort brought on by the oils Pana spread over his skin, Hateri was able to sleep fitfully throughout the heat.

At one point, he wanted to retrieve his pouches from across the room, but the muscles of his legs were balls of fire and the flats of his feet had been rubbed raw. The idea of moving that far made him ill.

At Eldoro's highpoint Chanzi delivered a meal, which Hateri ate.

When the cook returned for the tray, Hateri took advantage of the moment to ask for his pouches.

"Thank you," he said when the cook handed him the belts they were strung on.

Hateri dug into one worn pouch with two fingers and extracted the smooth rock that Pietha had given him the evening before they left Harshish Point.

The stone was cool, heavy in his palm. The surface had been etched with an impromptu image of the three hearts. Her smile as she gave it to him had contained the perfect balance of interest and mischief. The smooth surface of the stone brought him the full memory of the rest of that night.

"Consider it my fourth heart," she said to him later as she slid it over his bare chest.

"I don't have a fourth for you," he replied.

"Then you'll have to give me one of your three."

He thought of her kiss, warm in the cool chamber of the private section of the cave. He gazed out the window, into the hazy sky. Eldoro fell in the distance, and without needing to look he knew exactly where Katon would be. He thought about the old guide. Where was Taranth? Why had he left without a word for him?

Hateri chewed his lip.

He held Pietha's fourth heart in one hand, and threw the pouches across the room to skitter into the corner. Rolling the stone between his fingertips, he thought about what his father had asked.

Council member or not, his father was wrong.

Hateri was growing up in a different world. A new world where a Family member could be wrong, where Families were important but other things were, too. That's what they had proven out in the desert—all of them together, members of twelve Families. They had proven beyond doubt that the best way to survive was together, to have each other's backs regardless of their clan. He couldn't betray Pietha, or the rest for that matter. If his father couldn't understand that, it was not Hateri's fault.

The sky was growing dark by the time Hateri heard his father's voice outside his room. He clenched Pietha's heart in one hand and closed his eyes, bringing his blankets up over his shoulders to pretend sleep. The door opened and footsteps came closer. Stool legs shuddered across the floor before coming to a stop. The sound of his father's weight settling in was like judgment falling.

"I know you are awake."

Hateri turned to his back and stared at the ceiling.

"I told the Families that you found no Light That Fell from the Sky."

Hateri gritted his teeth and felt blood squeeze from his fingers as he clutched Pietha's stone. He was finally hungry, now, which was maybe good, but his mouth felt like it was pasted together.

"I am on your side, Hateri."

"No, you're not."

"You're not wrong—the Families should work together on this. But it's not time, yet."

"If not now, when?"

"I don't know, son. All I can say is that we will know it when it comes."

Hateri stared at the ceiling.

"I wish it were different. I really do."

Hateri remained silent.

"The Family heads want you to speak with them. I am delaying that as long as I can, but it's going to happen. And when it does, I need you to tell them that you found nothing. To say there is no Light That Fell from the Sky. Taranth told me you were headstrong, which I already knew. But he also said you were a leader, and that your friends loved you. If you don't support me on this, you will destroy the reason all of those friends died."

Hateri pressed his tongue against the roof of his mouth.

He shook his head.

"I can make it work," he said, forming each word clearly. "I have to make it work. I will show you that the Families can work together."

His father gave a sigh that dropped about half the weight in the world. He sat still for several moments, then left.

Hateri turned to his side again, pressed the smooth stone to his cheek, and tried to go to sleep.

Chapter 17

Jafred laid his head back against the door's hard surface.

The hallway outside his son's room was uncomfortably tight now, lit against the darkness with the cold glow of luminescent lamps made from crossbred moss grown in caves by three different Kandar Families. The arrangement between those Families was unique among the quadarti, the only truly collaborative effort between Families in existence prior to the expedition. It had taken nearly an entire season to work out—and that was between Families of the same clan.

The air that moved through the corridor was a result of a fanning system designed by the Waganat Family, and installed by the council over a year ago.

It galled Jafred now that he was no Waganat.

Ranya Waganat would just force his son to do what he said to do, and that would be it. But Jafred would rather face the disgrace of being barred from the council than take that kind of act. He could handle disgrace, as could Bethleen, his pair-mate and Hateri's mother.

As stubborn as Hateri could be, he was a grown quadar now. His son had to make his own choices.

Jafred pushed himself off the back of the door, and walked down the hall. He rubbed his chin, deep in thought as he passed through the door leading into the darkening night and out through the garden. He sat under the *grisa* tree, and took in the rest of the area, thinking of Bethleen and of the fact that she had chosen to remain on the northern slopes while he completed his tour with the council.

He held true affection for her, but her choice to remain in the slopes rather than be here with him showed how firmly her mindset was tied to that of the traditional Family order.

Bethleen would speak with Hateri, of course.

She would travel here as soon as she heard Hateri had been found alive. It would take time to arrive but she would come, and she would fawn over her son as any mother should. Since she had no knowledge that the Light That Fell from the Sky existed, her conversation would not be about that. Her words would carry only concern for her son's health, news about her own father, and the goings-on of the entire E'Lar Family. But merely by its focused exclusion of anything not Family or clan related, her rapid-fire conversation would carry the full impact of Families—exactly what Jafred needed Hateri to hear.

Unfortunately, her conversation would serve only to drive Hateri deeper into his position. Jafred had seen it before.

Her arrival was not going to help him here.

It would also force another conversation he didn't want to have.

His time on the council was due to finish at the end of this cycle, at which point he was intended to return to the northern slopes to join her. That had been the plan, anyway. It's what Bethleen had told all her acquaintances. Jafred didn't want to tell her he had decided to remain on the council seat for as long as they would have him.

She would ask why, and he wouldn't be able to tell her.

Unless, of course, Hateri proved good to his word, and exposed the existence of the Taranth Stone. If that happened, he would be returning to the north earlier than expected, anyway.

Jafred's problem was bigger than the Taranth Stone, though.

The reason he had decided to stay here in Esgarat City was bigger than even Hateri could comprehend right now.

Though his son was too distraught to hear it now, Jafred had come to the view that only by working together could the Families progress beyond their current state of living—that staying in the Esgarat basin was, in itself, limiting them. Harming them. In his opinion, the quadarti had to grow beyond the barriers of their world, or their civilization would strangle itself and slowly die.

He would have to try to explain his decision to Bethleen. But he could already hear her voice and see the edge to her central as she glared at him: *You're not going to tell me you believe the ravings of a few desert-baked philosophers, are you?*

But that is exactly what he believed.

He believed it because more than a few philosophers said it.

Medics explained about traits that passed through clans and Families. Scientists told him about the outsiders, quadars like Taranth who braved and survived in the harshlands outside the ring of Esgarat and proved that it could be done. Geologists revealed how the water reservoirs in the depths of the caverns that ran below might once have rushed across the lands, and how the ridges of the Esgarat itself may not have always been there.

And then there was Louratna, a teacher at the university where Hateri had been learning.

At first Jafred met with her to discuss his son's progress, but their conversations quickly bloomed. She was brilliant, and the fact that she worked in many fields meant she was able to tie things together in ways others could not.

As she matched her studies to others, shivers ran through his plates.

She had wanted to know how many quadars could live in the space of the Esgarat, so she gathered records from across history, and she laid her mathematics out on sheets of scrollwork. As is the way of scientists, her results made her ask more questions. She plotted root yields and leaf yields, apparent populations of *kax* and *piela* and the many types of flying *jah*. Against each of these she tallied every cycle's water yield, and noted as much information as she could gather on how those water levels changed in the deep caves under the One Great Esgarat around which the council city itself was built.

The message in her work was clear.

Disaster loomed if they couldn't find more space.

It might take generations, but Louratna's work showed events she called "decompressions" were not only possible, but as long as the quadarti remained inside the great ring, their population was almost guaranteed to go into one—a deep crash, a time when quadars would die off to almost nothing.

In fact, her report suggested that this had already happened to them, over a period of many thousands of cycles each time. Each such period saw their quadarti ancestors crawl from the caves, grow to a critical mass, then suddenly disappear into the safety of the underground once again. Each time was the same, just as Eldoro's passing was, but less predictable.

"Less certain," she said to him that last evening they were together. "The event itself is predictable, but the timing can be quite different each pass."

"Can we stop it?" he replied.

Her expression was not really an answer, but it was the closest to the truth he could imagine. Yes, that expression said. But, no.

He understood that expression much better now.

When he brought the work to the rest of the council, they laughed just as certainly as Bethleen would. The leaders of the Families would never make the kinds of adjustments—the kind of investments—needed. But knowing the facts, Jafred could not bring himself to leave his position now.

An expansion would not bring immediate profit, so the Families could not be trusted to think this way. The *council* must drive the quadarti to expand beyond the ring. Only the *council* could focus on what others might see as senseless exploration. Only the *council* could drive the Families and the clans together. Only the *council* was in a position to help the quadarti avoid the decompression that Louratna had proven to be somewhere in their future.

This is why the Families could not be trusted to study this Taranth Stone, also—whatever it was. The Light That Fell from the Sky was part of the answer he was looking for, the source to the decompression.

Jafred knew that the moment he saw it.

It had to be, didn't it?

If someone could discover its true nature, Jafred was as certain as he could be that this equipment would change the way they looked at the world.

Now he just needed to find a way to get Hateri to see this his way.

He took a deep breath, reveling in the quiet of the darkness in his garden.

Chapter 18

Two hands of heats passed before Hateri was fit enough to stand before the council, which is what he was now preparing to do. He waited at the back of the Greater Council chamber, watching the space fill up. His father—his da, as Taranth would have called him—was working the floor, playing the diplomat, his expression swinging from jovial to dour and back in the space of the flap of a *jah*'s wing. He wore his orange council robe, the lapels fabricated of the thick silk of rock spiders.

How apt.

The spiders wove tunnels of the stuff into the crevasses, tunnels that collected dew in the mornings and enticed their prey in to be feasted upon.

Politician, meet rock spider. Spider, politician.

Given that his father had been a council member for so long, and given that Hateri had grown up and gone to university here in Esgarat City, he had often imagined himself addressing this group. The reality of this moment, however, was nothing like his imaginings.

The chamber was crowded, and growing more so as heads of Families and their entire entourages filed in. Their footsteps and their hushed greetings reverberated against the walls of the stone chamber in such a great cacophony that it nearly drowned out his thoughts.

The quadars were here to get the full story of the expedition.

They wanted to hear about Yip Kil and Gis'le Ombat, Senni Gash and Jasneed Parity. The Dareh Family perched themselves on the front row, left, sitting in their golden robes of mourning, faces as firm as if they had been chiseled from the rock that made up the eastern slopes they called their homeland.

Attendance was not mandatory for any Family, but lack of attendance would show both regretful negligence and public disrespect for the dead of the most powerful Families in the community.

Hateri realized now that his talk would be half lecture, half eulogy.

He put his hand to his chest and felt the stone Pietha had given him underneath the cloth shirt he wore over his clean travel leggings.

It just seemed right that he come to the discussion dressed for the trail.

The stone pressed against his chest. The room, despite the crowd, felt empty somehow. The air tasted bland. The odor of the stone was dead. He took a breath and turned his head back and forth to ease his tension.

His central went to the M'ktals.

Pietha's mother was standing in the far corridor to his right. She was as tall as Pietha had been, but broader, wearing the same expression on her *witze*-oiled face that Pietha got when she was serious. It hurt him to look at her. Pietha's da was seated. His primaries and his central were all focused sharply on Hateri, his robes properly arranged, and his *witze* worn only over his skull and down the jawline as was traditional.

Hateri looked away, thinking about the work he did to place the stone Pietha had given him into a chain of pounded metals. If they loved her, they would have loved him, he thought, turning his gaze back to Pietha's da, and finding the edge of the elder's glare had not dulled.

Yes, he thought, *these Families mourned their losses grievously.*

And they would properly honor those who were lost.

When Hateri's father—his own da—introduced him, Hateri would tell the story fully and openly, giving the Families what they needed to finish their grieving and to see that to come together was to honor their children.

This was the way of the future.

They were ready for this. The death of his friends would be the flint that started the fire.

This idea burned in his chest, and nearly brought tears to his eyes.

He would see to it that his friends had died for something, and that something would be the thing that brought together their Families once and for all.

Hateri clasped his hands behind his back, and stood as tall as he could.

As he settled, his father stepped up the stairs to the podium and flagged the crowd to a silence broken only by the stray clacking of a throat or the random shuffle of bodies in seats.

"My friends and Families," Jafred E'Lar said. "We all know why we are here. As devastated as I am at your losses, I am nearly as ashamed at the joy I am filled with to say that my son is able to be here to speak with you. He has promised me in no uncertain terms that he will tell you nothing but the truth, because the truth—no matter how harsh that truth might be—is what is best for our world. So I request forgiveness in advance for him if his words cause any pain."

Jafred cleared his throat, then glanced at Hateri with a heavy expression.

Hateri flexed his hands, preparing to step forward, not certain what his father was attempting here. This wasn't the introduction he expected, but it would serve nonetheless. The thinly veiled admonition that cloaked his father's words would not change his testimony in the slightest.

"Before I have my son speak, however, I want to present a memorial that I and the rest of the council have commissioned to stand at the base of our chambers."

His father beckoned to the far side of the hall, and a pair of doors opened. Workers pushed and pulled a wheeled platform—three times as long as it was wide—across the chamber's polished floor. Hushed voices and the creak of wheels echoed in the open space. A large, lumpy object was on the platform, draped with sheets.

The audience edged forward on their seats.

When the platform arrived immediately center of the dais,

Hateri's father nodded to three of the service crew. They stepped to the platform and grabbed corners of the drapes.

"My friends," Jafred said loudly, "I give you the expedition."

The drape came off to the sound of rustling fabric.

When the reveal was complete, fourteen individual statues stood on the platform, each perhaps a bit more than half life-size, each depicting a member of the team.

A hush came over the chamber.

"When each of you entered," Jafred said, "you may have noticed the newly smoothed section of the chamber grounds before the steps that lead to this very chamber. It is the council's intention that, to honor the sacrifices of our Families, each of these representations will be affixed to that span."

Like the rest of the audience, Hateri viewed the statues.

Their faces were not perfect, but done well enough that they reminded him of places and moments: Hiva handing him a hammer to fix a board on the cart as they loaded it. Ogala blushing as she gave him a piece of her bread. Gis'le striding beside him.

He saw his own image and immediately hated it.

At the front of the party was something that was clearly supposed to be the gnarled shape of Taranth, but seemed to be nothing but a caricature. Hateri discerned no wisdom in the statue's expression, no nobility in its stature. He pressed his lips together to fight back a surprising burst of anger at both the artist and at Taranth himself.

He drew a breath and lingered on Pietha's statue, feeling almost as if the stone on his chest was being magnetically drawn to her.

Cestral's mother, Ellay of the Taler Family, came forward and touched the cheek of the figure that represented her daughter.

"I want to take this back," she said.

For too long of a pause Hateri heard only the sound of shuffling feet and awkward hesitation. All eyes went to Jafred.

"I understand your desire completely, Mother Taler," Jafred said. "But to take one piece away would…be…"

"She belongs on the east slopes," Ellay said, turning sharply toward Jafred. "You have your son. How can you keep this image of our daughter from us?"

"But—"

The head of the Kil Family spoke next. "We will take our figure with us, also. Yip Kil was a Kandar. She belongs in the east."

Voices burst in a wave then, a chaotic clamor of what might have been argument and dissent, or merely just anger and grieving.

"Ogala can come to the west with us," said a Tael.

"Likewise Pietha," said her father, his eyes flashing deep gold that reminded Hateri of her. The M'ktal motioned to his entourage, and they went to the platform to remove her figure.

Hateri's central constricted, and his jaw went slack.

He wanted to shout out as the M'ktal entourage huffed to lift Pietha's stone image, but no words would come. He took one step, but halted. It was like watching the killing fields at Harshish Point, but being without a gun.

He did not know what to do.

A flash of orange came from the podium, his father turning toward him, his council robes flowing with the momentum of his movement.

Do you see? his father's gaze said to him. *The Families cannot even honor their dead together. What makes you think they will act as one when it comes to the Taranth Stone?*

Hateri watched the chaos, as members of each Family took their piece of the collective. He didn't know what hurt most—that they were desecrating the very point of their Family members' deaths, or that his father had been right. Anger and loss burned through him to leave behind a cold, detached essence that reminded him of Taranth looking out over the horizon. The words came to him, then. *The desert takes what it wants.*

But Taranth was wrong—and in truth even Taranth knew he was wrong, though the gnarled old trail guide couldn't admit it. The desert had wanted Hateri. It had been ready to take him. But Taranth wouldn't let it. Taranth alone kept the desert from swallowing him when Hateri himself was unable to do it. Taranth alone had decided whether Hateri E'Lar would live or die.

Hateri looked at the statue that represented the guide.

Taranth had saved him.

"Enough!" Ranya Waganat pounded his staff on the floor to ring in silence. "Enough! I said."

When silence finally came, the head of the Waganats spoke again.

"I thank the council for creating the memorials. They will serve to make our Families stronger for our loss. But I remind everyone that we are here to listen to the young E'Lar tell his story about the trip, and to hear what he has to say about the Light That Fell from the Sky. I think we can wait to make final arrangements for the transport of our honorariums after we are finished with the young quadar's conversation."

The Families nodded and gave grumbles of agreement.

They gathered both their robes and their composure, and they made their way back to their positions. Their voices hushed again, and the shuffling of their feet quieted as they shifted and settled.

Hateri glanced at his father, who motioned him to continue, his gaze carrying the question that only Hateri could read.

He approached the platform. His first few steps were tentative and worried, but they grew stronger as he came to take his father's place at the podium.

The fourteen statues were all scattered now, twisted by the Families to face in haphazard direction, some already off the platform.

The point of Pietha's stone pressed against his breast, and he glanced to the artist's hunched representation of Taranth.

"I'm sorry to report," Hateri began, "that we were unable to find the Light That Fell from the Sky."

He saw his father's shoulders move with a deep breath.

Then he proceeded to tell the rest of the story, finding something each member of the team had done or said, reporting on valiant actions, and how they each played such important parts.

He related a joke that Yanil had told, and sang a snippet of a song Cestral had written after seeing Eldoro set in the wild lands outside.

It was, everyone agreed later, a beautiful eulogy.

After he was finished, and after the Families had voiced their approval, Hateri's father met him as he came off the podium. His expression was a mixture of relief and intensity that was hard to interpret, but the strength of the hug that came next was impossible to miss.

"I'm proud of you, son," his father said as he wrapped his arms around Hateri's shoulders. "I'm very proud of you."

Chapter 19

Taranth sat on his haunches in the depths of a cave far below the Esgarat.

He was hungry.

Merely sitting in the perfectly contoured gardens of the council member's household had been enough to remind him that he did not belong in Esgarat City. The smoothed surfaces of the brush in the council gardens were false to him. The shaped path of rounded rocks that meandered around the grounds held the sense of a sham. It all felt wrong in the way that even a well-intended lie was wrong.

When he left the city he thought he would go back to Harshish Point, but now he knew that idea was also folly. For him, staking claim to surface rock would be just as much a lie as the garden path was. Being where Alena had been could never replace being with Alena.

The truth of that fact settled harder than he expected.

The idea of being on the surface at all turned his stomachs sour.

Fighting the wind.

Working his way over the desert.

Setting water traps.

Hearing *neantha* bray and *piela* skitter across the rubble.

Those thoughts all brought back memories of young faces scrubbed raw by the sand, slack-jawed, heads thrown back, teeth dried and brittle as if they were screaming into the wind.

Five bodies laid out on the flats, waiting, the rest just gone.

The memories drilled into his mind like *drist* leeches through sand.

Life was nothing but hard, they said. Any beauty it held was both harsh and fleeting. A quadar lives life as it is, and then gives it up.

These were the facts.

Life is cruel, too.

For one instant life had let him think that he could change something, that maybe he could make a difference with those whelplings before he, too, was gone forever. For that brief time, Taranth had thought that what he did might actually matter.

Now all he had left for that idea were images of M'ran and four dead quadars who would never see a full cycle, all laid out on the desert floor, and the knowledge that he had lost even more who would never be found.

Now he baited a shiv of bent metal with a cave bug, and dipped it into the slowly running pool of cold water, looking to snag a fast swimming *kraun*, or perhaps one of the many-legged water lizards his central could pick out as they lay in the shallows. He watched the hook float to the bottom, twisting it gently as if the bug was injured and had just fallen from its perch.

He was tired, his muscles worn by the descent through slots and passages his da's da had shown him when he was even younger than the council member whelps.

His knees and the small of his back ached with age.

He didn't know how much longer he would live.

He didn't particularly care.

Time was different here, after all. It came in sleeps rather than heats. It came in the now.

The caves, like the desert above, took what they wanted.

Nothing he could do would change that, and simply living ached enough without making it worse by hoping for a future or by dwelling on a past.

All he wanted now was to snag his meal and slip into the sheltered slot he had found where he could rest.

When he *was* done, Taranth thought, when his life was over, he knew only that he would disappear silently back into the caves, alone and as invisible as either the whelps that his indifference had killed or the raider that his blade had given mercy to.

No one would care that he was gone.

No one would know.

He drew a breath of clean cave air and peered into the water.

He jogged the bait once more, coaxing in a *kraun*. When it struck, he pulled the fish onto the flat rock and beat it against the stone wall. When it was dead, he used his knife to prepare it.

When his meal was eaten, Taranth returned to his slot and lay against the wall, closing his eyes, and hoping that for this sleep, at least, he would not find himself dreaming.

The Taranth Stone

Chapter 20

"Do not take *no* for an answer," Hateri said to Unid.

The council server nodded.

They were in Hateri's office, which had been his father's office before him. It was nearly half a cycle ago that Jafred had passed. *Time is too fast*, Hateri thought as he looked at the wrinkles beginning to grow over his now-knobby hands.

Unid was a dependable and resourceful runner, with an intimidating aura about him. All of which were why Hateri had called for him on this chore. He was Kandar clan, also, which was helpful because Hateri did not want another Terilamat involved.

"I mean it," Hateri added as Unid gathered his council robes and crossed into the doorway. "He cannot refuse."

"I understand," the runner replied.

Then the door shut, softly but firmly.

Hateri stood up and went to the window. The simple opening spanned most of the wall. A doorway at the far end of the wall opened to the wide balcony, and a set of spiraling stairs led from the balcony down to the council gardens. Across the manor, the gate was closed.

He leaned his hands on the sill.

More than two cycles had passed since Taranth left a dried-up whelp on the doorsteps of that gate, and then disappeared into the night. No one had heard from him since, though Hateri knew of at least three clandestine efforts made by the more powerful Families to find him. Others had probably attempted, also, but Hateri had spent enough time with Taranth to know that if Taranth did not want to be found, he would not be found.

Not for the first time, Hateri wished he knew what had happened to his friend.

A clear spot in the clouds gave him purchase to see the red light of Katon, off kilter toward the west. Eldoro was a smudge in the cloud cover behind her.

He sighed and hung his head.

The skies had changed so much over the past cycle that many quadars were returning to the old gods. Where once there had been nothing but oranges and browns and gauzy covering, now sometimes that soft essence gave way to a flat blue when the sky was light and a hard blackness when the heats had set—and in the darkness the sky was riddled with patterned pinpoints of light that caused no little conversation.

The first rending was cataclysmic enough to bring life to a halt as quadars cowered in their homes. That it occurred in tandem with a steady increase in the amount of melting water that fell from the sky—drops laced with fiery liquid that slowly seeped through houses, destroyed plants, and ate away flesh—made the hysteria worse. Tiny Eterdane had been discovered then, a new heat, a tiny brightness too small to burn through clouds but brighter than the other points of light revealed when the clouds remained absent. Eldoro and Katon were shown for their true nature, massive balls of flame that burned behind the curtain of clouds.

Everything was changing.

Now, in the full darkness of Convergence, Eterdane gleamed in the blackness amid hundreds or, if philosophers were right, thousands of other glimmering points. Some of those philosophers were suggesting that perhaps Esgarat was the object that moved, not the heats themselves. One thought in particular was that both Esgarat and Katon circled Eldoro, giving rise to larger Eldoro's smooth path in relation to their home, and the more erratic movement of his sister.

Hateri sensed the danger in putting too much weight behind philosophers' opinions, though. They extrapolated answers from outside of the known, sometimes making claims as wildly unsupported as those of the church. As such, mainstream scientists viewed them with dubious eyes.

The turmoil diverted much of Hateri's attention from the problem his father had left him—fighting the decompression Louratna was still quite adamant about.

Now he had just come from a startling session.

"We cannot provide crops we don't have," the Banit Family messenger said to him, explaining the reasons behind reductions in the product being released and the increased prices for what there was. "The *havra* berries have come in worse each season for many years. The cold cycle starts earlier. And we need to fill our mouths, also."

"I understand," Hateri had said. "Tell your mother I appreciate everything she is doing to increase her yields."

The news meant he would not be able to send the colonies the amounts he had promised, but even the reduced amounts were better than nothing. The colonies had been his father's pride. They were operating well and thriving as best as could be expected. Hateri had gone to one of the outposts just before his father had passed, and seen for himself it was nearly a real civilization—a nicer place for a free-range quadar to live than Harshish Point had been, though admittedly still rough in comparison to the Esgarat.

The news also meant that he couldn't wait any longer to change the way the science teams were working.

Hateri thought of his father.

Jafred E'Lar had been right, of course.

The Families couldn't be trusted to examine the Taranth Stone.

But the restraints required to keep the existence of the stone completely secret had slowed their work at every step. For example, Hateri had continued his father's practice of interviewing each scientist himself to discern the depth of their ties to the Families. It took patience and it took time, but it was worth it.

The lines of lies and secrets had grown massively complex over the years. Hateri didn't think their deception would hold much longer. He was amazed it had lasted as long as it had.

Now, though, he wondered if all the chaos could be tied together. Was it a coincidence that the clouds disappeared after the Taranth Stone arrived outside Esgarat? Was the burning rain connected? What were the heats, really? Did someone there send them the Taranth Stone, and if so, why?

All he knew for sure was that nothing he had done so far had worked, so it was time to take a different approach.

At least, that's what he thought.

"I hope I'm doing the right thing, Father," he said aloud as he took in the garden and arched his back.

Yes, he was getting old.

He glanced back to the gate, sighed, then left his office to make his way to the chambers.

CHAPTER 21

The door opened and the chime rang. A delivery runner's engine sputtered as it labored past.

The quadar who entered Baraq Waganat's shop wore the orange robe and obsidian jewelry of the Quadarti Council. His skin was leathery and brown. He smelled of *kadea* oil. The yellow orbs of his primaries blinked with iridescence in the shop's dimness, his central a crystal blue orb high on his forehead that marked him as from the eastern regions. He stepped through an aisle, gliding past a row of hand tools. A mobile of gliders spun lazily near his head.

Baraq's three hearts beat rapidly, chilling his wrinkled skin.

A hand-tall stack of accounts to be paid sat in a sloppy pile on his counter, and the ledger he was filling was only halfway complete. *Wonderful*, he thought morosely as he looked at the council's runner. *I needed something else to do.*

He glanced to where his weapon lay waiting. It was a recent-model Tegra, acquired in trade for diverting a shipment of root, a good gun with lots of stoppage but less than accurate at longer ranges. Crissandr despised the weapon, of course, and hated that he kept it loaded and in such easy reach. "No one will touch a Waganat," she explained. But desperation leads to a certain lack of caution, and a Family name is good for only so much.

He liked something else about the gun, too, something he would never tell Crissandr. The gun made him feel independent, his own man, separate from and unreliant upon his Family.

The runner approached the counter, surrounded by the billowing odor of spices and sulfur. He pulled his upper lip back in a smile, showing yellow teeth that matched his now-slim irises.

"You will come," the quadar said.

"Hello to you, too, my friend."

"You will come."

"I'm quite busy," Baraq said, pointing to his paperwork.

"Paper can be shuffled anytime."

"I cannot leave. Who will run my business?"

The runner gazed around the empty shop. "Your aisles overflow with customers. Maybe you should purchase a larger building."

Baraq shrugged. "It is a slow moment."

The runner put six-fingered fists on the counter and leaned forward. His jewelry glinted. The heavy ridge above his primaries bulged together like a distended sand worm.

"You come."

A hackle clawed its way up Baraq's spine. Despite being far down the line of succession and nearly invisible to his Family's power structure, he was still a Waganat. He could send the council's runner away. But they would then make things difficult. It was best not to trifle with them if it could be avoided.

"Just a moment," Baraq said.

He went to the back of the store and engaged a series of switches.

Metal bars fell across windows. Levers clanged into place.

He had installed the device during the last Convergence, when the heat light of Eldoro and Katon traveled together, leaving the sky dark at night. He remembered the timing because the clouds had broken often then, and the temperature had fallen so far during the darkness that pools of water actually formed on the ground in the mornings.

"I'm ready," he said.

The runner nodded, then led him away.

The council chamber was a tall, rounded room that smelled of influence and was ringed with columns of gray-veined basalt that rose to a rounded ceiling open at the center. Katon's highpoint neared, and the smaller of the two heats was a hazy blot glaring through the opening. Eldoro had risen, but was too low to be seen in the chamber. The floor was flat rock inlaid with a spiral of shining obsidian from the foothills of Holy Esgarat.

Baraq had expected to see the council in session.

Instead, only Councilor Hateri E'Lar greeted him, his ceremonial robes wrapped about him as if they were armor. His hairless skull was nearly perfect in its roundness, dimpled only at the back of his parietal temple. His primaries were pinpoints of the darkest brown.

Despite his hearts pounding, Baraq kept a disdainful grace to his stride as he approached the councilor. "What do you want?" he said.

"Greetings to you, too," Hateri replied dryly.

"You are the last councilor I would expect to arrange a personal meeting with a Waganat."

"Come, Baraq. Let's not get mired in trivial arguments."

Hateri was a proponent of quadarti regulation. Every session saw him propose new constraints on trade and new taxes on materials. This was not something the Waganat Family was pleased with, and grumbling about Hateri E'Lar was a common occurrence when any two Waganats found themselves together.

"Open trade may be a triviality to you, but it is life to me," Baraq said.

The councilor's face betrayed no emotion. "I'm sure the Waganats would get by under any rules set forth."

"What does my Family have to do with this?" Baraq replied with more anger than he meant to reveal.

"Nothing, Baraq. Absolutely nothing."

"Well then, what am I here for?"

Hateri motioned with one arm. "Follow me, please."

Without waiting, the councilor stepped into a long hallway.

Baraq followed in uncertain silence.

After several corridors, a lift ride to lower levels, and more corridors, they came to a set of double doors.

Hateri turned to the guard.

"I think will be fine from here," he said.

The quadar clicked his understanding, and faded away, his sandaled footsteps rustling in the empty hallway.

Hateri motioned Baraq forward.

The small room beyond the doors was filled with cabinets, a

long table, and several chairs. A row of brown smocks hung from hooks on the wall.

"Grab a covering," Hateri said, pulling one over his robes. He put a key to another door.

Baraq felt like a whelpling as he did as he was told.

That was his lot in life. Do as you are told. Follow in the lines. He was past half-age, well beyond the time when he might do something new, past the time where quadars around him expected brilliance.

When Baraq was ready, Hateri pushed the last door open.

A dry odor of camphor came from all directions.

The lab was almost as large as the council's chamber, but where the council's home was garnished and ancient, this room was an austere grid of tables, machinery, and test panels with rows of glass bulbs that glowed xenon colors. Diagrams and sketches were gummed to the walls. The item that drew his attention, however, sat on a row of tables lashed together. The thing was huge and brown, long and rounded, easily several times as long as Baraq was tall.

He stepped forward.

Its shell was pebbled like a lizard's skin, broken and torn apart in places. Inside were boxes with green and white and black connection wires protruding from them.

"What is it?"

Hateri's grin was bright as cloudless Eldoro at highpoint. "Can you not guess?"

Baraq glanced back at the table.

The thing's shape was sleek and bulletlike, its nose smashed, its tail open and blackened. Baraq's hearts pounded. Parts of the shell had been ground away. Components lay scattered in controlled patterns.

He tenderly ran a webbed finger along the thing's surface.

"The Light That Fell from the Sky?" Baraq said.

Hateri clicked from the back of his throat, obviously enjoying Baraq's incredulity.

"It has been a long time since we've called it that."

"What do you call it now?"

"The Taranth Stone," he said, raising a hand when Baraq showed confusion. "Don't worry, I'll tell you the story sometime."

Baraq did not press the question.

He knew that more than a cycle ago—maybe thirty years—a searing ball of flame had scorched the nighttime sky beyond the Esgarat range. The council had sent a party to search for it, as had the Waganat Family. But thirty years ago, the Family's machines were unreliable and incapable of completing the trip. By the time they arrived, the mountain's volcanic landscape had shifted to cover whatever secrets the site may have provided. All of the party—including his own uncle—had perished, except for the guide and except for Hateri E'Lar.

At least that was the story.

That didn't stop rumors from building, though.

Esgarat, the tallest mountain peak on the continent, was thought to be the place their species first emerged from the caves to walk the surface, so the priests proclaimed it was no surprise that the holy light was seen there. It was only fitting, they said, that the gods would send fire to the place of the quadarti origin. They claimed the light would bring Eldoro's power to Esgarat, and that it had the ability to strike enemies with rays of death.

Scholars debunked those claims and suggested the ball of flame was more likely just a trick of the clouds, reflecting a storm or other distant light in a spectacular fashion.

Amid the heated spiritual battles was another intriguing story, one that said that the original expedition had actually succeeded in their quest, and that a plainsguide named Taranth had found the remains of a great stone and hauled it to a place of safekeeping.

"How did it come to be here?"

Hateri waited.

"You've had it here all along?"

"We wanted to study it."

"Likely story."

"Nonetheless, true."

"Nonetheless, I doubt it."

Baraq fought a flickering anger. Bureaucracy delays progress, and it was saying something that this was among the most egregious examples he had seen.

"Either way, the end result is still withholding the existence of the stone from the public."

"It's not a worse deal than your Family would have given."

In that, Baraq had to admit the councilor was right. His Family developed technology and sold it to the highest bidder. It was an ugly field, one that tied progress to financial reward. The councilor's statement was true in that way, that the Waganat Family was really no better than the council, withholding beneficial inventions until the price was right.

"Why am I here?" Baraq asked.

"Why do you think you're here?"

Baraq thought for a moment. The room hummed with the heavy sound of a floor fan. The lab was empty, he realized. No one was working.

"The thing is obviously a device of some sort."

"True," Hateri replied patiently.

"So, somebody had to make it."

"Again, quite astute."

"You haven't been able to figure out how it works," Baraq said, the truth dawning.

Hateri smiled. "We've made progress, of course. Instructor Geldour-enet and his assistant have learned much about its aerodynamics through modeling. The university is working with an advanced heat-bearing composite based on the outer shell's chemistry. We've got a student developing approaches to power generation based on the system's configuration. None of these teams know the origins of these ideas though."

Baraq focused his central on the councilor. "What kind of power systems are they creating?"

"I'm just a politician, Baraq. You'll have to ask someone who understands all that."

"So, what's the problem?"

Hateri sighed hollowly. "The problem is the same as it has been since my father's time, Baraq. The problem is us. Or maybe better stated, the problem is me."

"You?"

"Because of my edicts, the council limits who can know what," Hateri said. "And the council can no longer agree what to do. Jie-Kandor O'Lat, who as you surely know is our representative from the Kandar clan, will not accept less than debating where we send each subsystem for study, then he bogs us down with reasons why his sector should do all the examinations. Asha Denari, of the

Hlrat, thinks that, as the device came from her region, her scientists should be allowed to discover how it works. We do not tell the aligned churches as much, but they merely wish to bury all such investigations—although the Prime Dias of Eldoro sees the idea of the stone as proof that the creator exists outside the sky, and is petitioning to use it as an icon for his services."

Baraq clicked his throat as he examined the Taranth Stone again. "And all the while the system sits waiting," he said.

Hateri nodded. "The sphere of quadars in the know grows, though."

"You fear its existence will be compromised."

"Yes. But more important, every moment we lose in determining how it works leaves those who made this that much further ahead of us."

Baraq gazed at the councilor, sensing something deeper to his comment. "You're afraid of them?"

"In addition to our examinations, my father also chartered thought studies and other experiments to discover where it might have come from. The council has searched everywhere, Baraq. For nearing two cycles we've been thinking of everything we could take in. We thought we knew everything there was to know about the world, right? We thought we had discovered all there is to discover. But then," he motioned to the device, and shook his head. "We find a device of mysterious power developed by someone we cannot find. And afterward the sky opens and the clouds change. Wouldn't you be afraid?"

"What do you want me to do about it?" Baraq said.

Hateri's pupils gleamed blackly in the room's light. "I can arrange to ship pieces of the device to you. I want you to use whatever contacts you think are best for whatever study you undertake."

"You want me to…work on it?"

"I want you be the science coordinator. I want you to discover what you can. I want you to expedite the study."

The device lay on the table before him in a different light now.

Baraq could almost hear it whisper, luring him, seducing him like rock fates tempting Mandrath in tales his mother had once told him. Reason spoke inside him, though. The Waganats did not develop technology for any but themselves. It was more than a policy. It was an oath that ran in his Family's veins as surely as did their blood. If he took this job, it would cause a rift.

"My Family—"

"Your Family is there, and I expect you will use your connections wisely. But given what I've said of the politics regarding the device, you see why they cannot participate."

"No, I don't."

"Your Family would attempt to control its results and would hold its benefits ransom."

Baraq was taken aback.

"Why me, then?" he asked.

"I've been watching you. You're a good quadar. You care about our society and you respect technology. In that sense you are better than the rest of your Family, you know?"

Hateri's expression grew serious.

Given the council member's reputation, Baraq wasn't sure how to take the compliment.

"But you are a technology person, too," Hateri said. "You are an inventor at heart. Look at this device. You see what it means, don't you? You see how much we can gain from it."

Baraq never cared for politics. What he loved, what kept him rising from his pallet every morning to work in his grungy little shop, was the idea of understanding how things worked. Now Hateri was offering this chance to study what was quite possibly the greatest technological discovery of all history.

A chill crossed Baraq's skin.

"You're choosing me because I am invisible, aren't you?"

"I won't begin our relationship by lying," Hateri said. "That you have not risen to the level you deserved is a benefit. But I would also suggest that you have remained of lower stature within your Family because you are more engineer than businessman—and that is a bigger benefit to me."

Baraq flashed on the image of his father scowling at him.

"What if I turn you down?"

"I've spent a very long time on this decision," Hateri said quietly as he traversed the Taranth Stone. "If you turn me down, I'll have to find someone else and I'll have to trust that you won't give my project away." He picked up a diagram, then placed it carefully down, crossed his hands in front of himself, and scanned the device laid out on the table. "But I wasn't lying earlier. I've watched you. I've assessed who you are. I don't think you'll turn me down."

Baraq pressed his lips together, and clicked his throat as he swallowed.

He shouldn't do this. But the idea of returning to his shop to face the pile of bills fell over him, and he let his gaze fall longingly on the Taranth Stone as it lay before him, making his hearts pump blood chilled with acidic energy.

"I'm sure we can work something out."

The words slipped from his tongue before he realized he had even thought them.

Chapter 22

Hateri left him with the Taranth Stone for the rest of the heat.

Baraq poked and prodded. He studied diagrams and devoured the layout. The device was elegant in its own fashion, beautiful in its own way. He took it in, trying to understand the minds of the creatures who had made it. As Hateri had all but suggested, they were not quadarti. That much was certain.

The way the wiring looped through the device described them as efficient but generous. The way the system's weight appeared unevenly distributed judged them perhaps a bit hasty in their action. The sharp flavor of knowledge oozed from every component, a taste full of intrigue and fear and flat-out envy.

He considered keeping the study to himself.

He wanted to do it all, of course.

But he knew this was beyond his capabilities, and he already understood that Hateri had chosen him more for his contacts and his sense of the whole than any particular skill he might have—a fact Baraq found he could suddenly live with. The quadars Baraq chose to work on this project would have to be the best in their fields, though, and they would have to operate under the guideline of silence until the entire effort was finished.

By the time Hateri returned for him, he knew what he was going to do.

One of the more interesting pieces of technology here was a series of smooth-walled chambers connected by necked orifices.

The assembly filled what he thought of as the rear of the device. This, Baraq would give to Kaatla Regonar. Kaatla was pioneering a flying craft, and he understood engines. He also knew how to be silent when the time came.

A box filled with metallic etchings and multicolored wafers would go to Estaut, a friend from his time at the university who had designed electronic circuits almost from the time he was born.

And finally, Baraq would provide the last item, a package that had been bolted onto a sliding bay door inside the Taranth Stone's underbelly, to Louratna. Its cylindrical system was made of a white material he had never seen before. Inside were more of what he took to be electronics and a collection of hourglass-shaped components that were linked like wheel spokes. A cracked light bulb sat in the center, and a twisted ring of tarnished metal was wrapped around the wheel's circumference giving the hourglass components bare clearance.

If anyone could figure out what this was, it would be Louratna, an old quadar who had taught him how to think, and how to see things in places that others would miss. From her he received many of his greatest lessons, and he was certain that she knew far more about things in the world than he could ever truly understand.

Chapter 23

Eldoro's heat was a red blot on the horizon when Baraq finally went home. The clouds had broken on the dark side of the sky.

When he was younger those clouds had been an ever-changing but constant blanket—light tan and gray and orange in the heated hours and an inky brown or red in the darkness. The heats of Eldoro and Katon were thought to be just that, massive blobs of heat energy that flowed through the clouds like a fish swims in the sea. But that changed when the clouds parted.

Eterdane's appearances still drew crowds, and as Baraq strode home late that night, a gathering formed on a slope of basaltic rock, staring at the smallest heat with slack-jawed wonder.

"Three heats for three hearts," a female in white robes said from a hastily constructed podium. "It is a new heat, I say. A holy time. Come with us as Eterdane grows to her rightful place and takes her seat with Eldoro. Be blessed in the growing warmth of our goddess as she replaces Katon."

Rubbish, Baraq thought, scowling.

Such misguided hash had no place in rational thought.

Three heats in the sky had nothing to do with the fact that quadars had three hearts. The world was hot, and a quadar's blood was used both to pass oxygen to the body as well as to cool it. Each heart absorbed heat and returned it to the atmosphere via plates on the quadar's shoulder blades. Everyone knew that. If a secondary heart failed, the quadar was more likely to die of heat exposure than of a lack of oxygen.

Still, the quadars who gathered around the priestess nodded at her distortions.

These were strange times.

Change comes hard, and things were changing faster than they had ever changed before. The idea of the Families working together, for example, might never really take. His father railed heavily against such discussion, though he had made inroads in selling the council several technologies for extracting water from the ground to support the three common communities the E'Lars had driven so hard to build outside the ring.

But Baraq couldn't help being upset at opportunism that sprang up so readily amid both philosophers and church.

Religious portents like this quadar's preaching made his stomachs clench, and the lack of credibility of the raw environmentalists who warned about their world cooling to ice at the same time as an ocean of burning liquid was falling from the sky gnawed at his sense of dignity. Philosophers extrapolated the existence of other worlds and talked of travel to them. Beleaguered scientists, of course, were just trying to figure everything out.

Baraq liked data.

His money had always been on the scientists.

He glanced at Eterdane, high in the night sky.

It was a small heat, a pinprick of bright light unable to be observed except during brief moments when the clouds parted in just the right way. With a little data, scientists had been able to ascertain Eterdane's movement was erratic and similar to Katon's rather than circular about the world as Eldoro's was. And, the priestess's ranting prophecies notwithstanding, Eterdane seemed to neither grow nor fade. Her path was predictable.

Yes. Predictable.

That's what you did with data.

Baraq was too tired to think about it right now, though.

Despite that fatigue, his mind filled with thoughts of the device hidden in the council's secret network of buildings. He pictured its wires and boxes, asked himself questions about materials of types he had never seen. For the first time in a very long time, Baraq realized he was humming.

He went straight to the kitchen.

"I'm glad you made it home," Crissandr said. She was seated at their table, reading the news roll delivered earlier.

He smiled. "Me, too."

No matter what happened throughout the heat, a single word or sometimes merely a glance from Crissandr made things better.

She wore a red *haldi*, a robelike dress that clasped at the side. It had been a favorite style of her mother's, a staple of the Festia Family that was her birthright. Her central was flecked with green, and her head and face were rounded and perfectly formed, her lips full and graceful in the manner of females.

"There's *havra* and *jaran* in the box."

He pulled his dinner from the retainer. "How long ago did you eat?"

"A while. I was hungry. I'm sorry I didn't wait."

"I'm glad you didn't."

"Working on something important? Or did you just get caught up and lose time?"

He chewed his food, savoring the coarse taste of the *havra* and ignoring the fact that he knew it was getting to be expensive. There was something about Crissandr tonight. Her face crinkled with an anxiety he could spot from paces away.

"What is it?" he asked.

Crissandr put her book down and took one of his hands. Her eyes softened and her irises dilated.

"We're going to have a child, Baraq."

Hara ran toward him, her tiny arms outstretched. She jumped, and he caught her, swinging her in the air as she giggled. She had been only six.

He closed his eyes, surprised at the crispness of his memories. He could still feel his daughter's tiny body against his chest. She had been dead for over three years.

"You saw her just then, didn't you?"

Baraq drew a breath. "Yes."

He didn't tell her that his next thought was of the Family—his father parading over his child's *jahalarat*, overseeing the process of bringing another Waganat into his clutches, looking at the child like the prospective laborer it would certainly be, like another of so many slaves.

"Not a heat goes by that I don't think of her."

"Me, too," Crissandr said, her voice wavering between anxiety and guilt, her central clouding. "I think it's all right, though, don't you?"

When he was younger, he would never have understood the power he had at this moment, the ability to crush his pair-mate with a single word or to raise her up with a mere glance. The muscle over her brow was tight, and her lips were now drawn and bloodless. But hope flooded her primaries, and she held her body upright and forward, bold and proud like a warrior marching.

He nodded and smiled warmly. He kissed her lips, tasting her fear as it slipped away.

"It's better than all right."

Inside, though, his stomachs twisted and he felt the clutches of his Family name, saw images of Hara, and oddly—so oddly—smelled the arid chill of skies littered with blue-white pinpoints glimmering.

CHAPTER 24

The year moved through Convergence and into Divergence—when Eldoro and Katon ruled opposite sides of morning and night—then to the time of Eldoro Leading, when the heat of that god rose early to be chased through the sky by his smaller sister.

Crissandr began to show signs of their child.

They did the sacrifices to ask aid in preparing their home for the child's arrival, twelve bows to the greater heat and six to the lesser. They attended a Family outing, Baraq cringing when the topic of the *jahalarat* was brought up.

Part of his discomfort was the Taranth Stone, of course, which he studied at night when he could slip away.

He decided that the next piece of technology he looked at would be a device that appeared to shoot light into another box of strange components. He wanted to talk to someone about it. He wanted to share the wonder of his findings. But his first three experiments were not complete, and he didn't want to stretch himself too thin.

So he waited.

He was repairing a wall in his shop when he learned Kaatla Regonar had crashed and died in one of his flying machines.

Kaatla had recently briefed Baraq on his progress. The system, he said, was designed to push the Taranth Stone through the air at great speed. The basic dynamics of the process was similar to those that propelled a bullet from a gun, but different: Fuel burned in a small compartment exhausted through a nozzle, resulting in a force in the opposite direction. Still, the equations that governed the process remained a mystery, as did anything about what kind of fuel the device used. Kaatla had sent a sample of the inner compartment to a cohort for analysis, but had not heard back at the time of their meeting. In the meantime, he was experimenting with his own shaped chambers.

Kaatla's death was a setback, but Baraq thought nothing strange about it at the time. Kaatla was a risk-taker, a trait that made him the inventor he was. He had been working on his flying machine for years, and quadars had been predicting a broken neck for just as long.

Two heats later, Estaut's pair-mate found Estaut floating in an underground pool.

He, too, had just briefed Baraq, reporting that the wafers seemed analogous to the quadars' own component-driven electronics, and that microscopic examinations of each component revealed a vast collection of circuitry. He had been able to excite small pieces of the device, but had no way to probe the wafers themselves and did not understand how such a component might be built. The next step would be running studies of the material to see if something could be learned from it.

But Estaut was dead the next heat.

A cold shiver came over Baraq.

He went to the room where he had heard from both of the now-dead scientists. A round table sat in the room's center. He stepped quietly about, looking under the table and chairs and lifting decorations from the wall. He found what he was looking for behind a rendition of Eldoro chasing Katon across the sky, blue bolts of lightning encircling both.

A wave talker was embedded in the middle of the lower frame rail, placed there so as to avoid throwing the image out of balance. Wires led to thick battery packs in each corner.

Ironic, he thought. The rendition had been one of his personal favorites. Now it was forever ruined.

Two quadars were dead because of him.

And he knew exactly who had done it.

"You killed them," Baraq said, controlling his anger.

His father folded his hands over his belly. His face was rounded and jowly, his skin hanging from his cheekbones like molten slides of flesh. Ranya Waganat was becoming an old quadar.

"Why do you say that?"

"Because they both died shortly after briefing me, and because of the wave talker you have in my office. No one else has wave talkers, Father. I'm sure you understand that."

The story was legendary inside their Family, yet unspoken of outside.

Some years ago, Jarka'el Waganat, Baraq's cousin a few times removed, had developed a machine that sent and received encoded waves of energy that could be descrambled with an appropriate receiver. It was a monstrous machine that created waves of incredible power. He demonstrated the device by sending a message asking his pair-mate to make *havra* stew for dinner. The Family's fortune had been made through negotiations, and they didn't need schooling to recognize power in the ability to speak rapidly via invisible waves.

In a discussion that raged for weeks, the Family decided to keep the wave talker for themselves rather than sell it.

They had improved it over time, learning to boost power and focus the waves, and learning to use higher frequencies where waves could be made to carry voice more readily than the irregular, massively powerful spark-generated waves of Jarka'el's first machine. They doled out systems within the Family when it suited them, using wave talking as bargaining levers for critical contracts and other business advantages.

"You should have known better than to develop technology for the council, Baraq," his father finally replied.

"It was work."

"You should have come to me."

Baraq remained silent.

"We've had this discussion before," his father said. "You have your business because of the Family. You have your life, your wealth, and your home because of the Family. Don't choose this time to forget that."

Baraq cringed.

He was far removed from any real power within the Family, and he always would be. He considered telling his father off. He thought of exposing him, going to the full public with the existence of this glorious device that could be used to spy on others. He thought about the danger that would befall his father if he did that. Then he thought about Crissandr and his soon-to-come child.

I'm drowning, Baraq thought. *As certainly as Estaut did in the caves, I'm drowning.*

His father spoke.

"You will tell Hateri that you can find nothing of worth."

Baraq's stomachs dropped. "You know who funds me."

His father gave a nonchalant shrug. "Hateri will be discredited shortly."

"What do you mean?"

"You think the rest of the council doesn't know he's broken from their ranks?"

"You told them?"

"That's what partners do."

The sentence settled fully.

"Does that surprise you? Did you really believe the council actually ran this city unilaterally?" his father said. "Did you think we don't care?"

"No," Baraq said. "Not really."

Baraq's insides tried to rise up and clog his throat. A fire burned over his skin.

For much of the past year he had felt alive. He was studying the Taranth Stone, doing something important. And for once he was working on his own. At least, he thought he had been. Now he realized once again that he was no more than a *drist* leech, a sand worm. Useless, meaningless. Removed from the structure of his Family, unable to affect its decisions, unable to break from their clutches, and too weak to buck them.

"How big of a cut do they get in return for laws that keep others at bay?"

His father laughed with a smile full of yellow teeth. "You have grown into a good businessman, Baraq."

"How big?"

"Big enough."

Baraq considered recent events. How much did his father know of Louratna? She did not travel from her home and would not visit Baraq's office, so their discussions had been away from the prying wave talker.

"So, two quadars are dead, and you will discredit Hateri."

"Yes."

"What about me?"

"What about you?" His father's eyes were level and unwavering now, their challenge firmly placed. If Baraq let this go, he could continue to run his shop, continue to go home to sleep each night. But the Family would protect itself. Wave recorders. Spies. Inspections. He would never know from one moment to the next when someone was watching him. And if he did not let this go, Baraq saw the result in his father's eyes.

Though no one would say it aloud, the Waganats were not above disposing of their own if necessary.

"What will happen to the Taranth Stone?"

His father smiled. "Do not fear, Baraq. The time is coming for it to make its public appearance. We will continue the investigation and will bring any useful discoveries to market, just as we always have."

"I understand, Father," Baraq said.

And he understood something else, too. His father did not know of Louratna's work.

Chapter 25

Hateri entered the smaller of the three council meeting chambers just as he always did, running just a touch late as he almost always was, and wearing his council robes which he also almost always did.

"I apologize for my lateness," he said as he opened the doors and stepped in.

Jie-Kandor was there, as was Asha. They were the council members selected from the Kandar and Hlrat clans. Both were due to be out of their terms at the end of the cycle.

Four other service members were there, however, which was not per usual. They stood stiffly upright, their primaries on edge. Unid was one of the four. Hateri cast a question in his gaze, but the runner gave no indication.

"What have I missed?" Hateri said as the door swung shut.

"The better question is, what have *we* missed?" Jie-Kandor said. He was as still as the runners.

"I don't understand."

"I'm sure that is not correct."

"I see," Hateri said, suddenly understanding why he had not heard from Baraq Waganat for a considerable time. "This is about the Taranth Stone."

"We thought all actions regarding the stone were to be decided by the three of us," Asha said.

Hateri considered his position.

"I won't lie," he said. "I was afraid we were not moving fast enough."

The door opened behind him. The bent form of Ranya Waganat stepped through, moving in a fashion that reminded Hateri of old L'rdent from Harshish Point. Hateri had not thought of that place or those quadars in a long time. He wondered if L'rdent was still alive.

"Elder Waganat," Hateri said in greeting.

Ranya nodded, then sat at a table with such deliberate effect that the full depth of what was happening fell over him. His game was over. The Families would have the Taranth Stone.

"What's going to happen to Baraq?" he said.

"We will deal with him inside the Family," Ranya said.

"I see."

"You, on the other hand, are a different problem."

Hateri saw that Jie-Kandor and Asha were taking a back seat now, and that said only one thing.

"You're here to remove me as the Terilamat selectee," he said.

"You will be allowed to resign."

"And if I don't?"

Ranya gave a hand movement that said he didn't care either way. "Once the rest of the Terilamat clan hears of your deceit, they will decide it's time we had fresh blood in the office and you will be shunned."

The answer told him everything.

Leave quietly, and Ranya Waganat would take over the councillorship, including proprietary control of the Taranth Stone. The salvage would be kept together because then the Waganats could control it all. Oh, sure, Jie-Kandor and Asha would have fingers in it, but Hateri had seen what the Waganats did. In short order, Ranya would have Jie-Kandor and Asha so confused that Ranya's would be the only fingers that mattered.

Make a fuss, though, and the full truth would come out.

And if the full truth came out, the Taranth Stone would not remain together.

He made a click at the back of his throat, and realized it didn't matter.

Ranya Waganat wouldn't keep the Taranth Stone together even if he held control of the entire thing. He was in business. He would do what the business needed.

This was over.

He had failed.

The weight of the elder Waganat's stare said everything that had happened since the expedition was announced was finished now. The twelve. Taranth. His father. Even M'ran. Hateri had failed them all. The only open question was whether he would step down in silence or be subject to discredit.

"I see," he said.

"I suggest that perhaps you might want to spend the rest of your time in one of your father's colonies," Asha said.

"I have already arranged for such passage for you," said Jie-Kandor. "I've asked the support staff here to escort you to your quarters to pack the few things you might need on the way."

Hateri's central caught the gentle nod of Unid's head.

"Convenient," he said to Jie-Kandor. "Almost like you planned to get me completely out of the way."

"Almost," Jie-Kandor replied.

"All we need now," Ranya Waganat said, "is your resignation."

Hateri wrapped his fingers around the back of the chair in front of him, and bowed his head. Worse things existed than living out the rest of your useless life in a colony that your father had built, but very few worse things than knowing you could do nothing to save the whole of your species.

"You have it," he said, sealing his defeat. "I resign my commission to the council."

Chapter 26

Crissandr's belly swelled as time passed.

Baraq worked in his shop, selling automatic door openers and machines that served food. Each transaction sent money to the Family and a slice to the council. With every good sold, Waganat control fueled more Waganat control.

He wanted to contact Louratna. Every heat he told himself that he would try, but someone from the Family was constantly loitering around his shop, and he told himself that he could not risk causing her a similar fate as Kaatla and Estaut. The truth, though, was that he was more afraid for himself than for Louratna.

Heats passed as Katon caught slowly up to her brother, bringing chills to the darkness when Baraq walked home and skies that were sometimes cloudless and sharp.

On one such night a dark form stopped Baraq.

"Come with me," it whispered with feminine softness. She grabbed his arm and pulled him along.

Baraq's hearts pounded. "Why? What's going on?"

"No time," the intruder replied fervently. "Come now."

She pulled him through several tight streets and then behind a row of buildings.

Soon, he found himself in the small candle-lit cellar of a shop. It was a spare chamber, one wall still barren earth, the rest made of mortared brick. A female sat behind a simple table, draped in a robe of coarse cloth.

"Louratna," he said.

She wore a headdress of twined *katja* that rested on her knobby head in several places. She looked at him with her unshakable demeanor as if they were merely sitting together in the middle of the bazaar and not as if he had just been essentially kidnapped.

The device he had given her sat on the table before her.

"Good evening," she replied in her throaty voice.

"I'm sorry I haven't contacted you," he explained rapidly. "But, there have been…complications."

"Complexities are bound to arise."

"What do you mean?"

"What did you suspect when you gave this to me?"

Baraq's smile had the flavor of self-congratulation to it.

His father would never have brought someone like Louratna into this study. Nor would Hateri have, though Baraq understood the council member had studied under her.

Louratna was a mathematician.

She had studied in the university under Hunta Askalin, the male who had developed an understanding of numbers in an imaginary plane. But she was a philosopher, also, something she had proven to Baraq during long discussions they had held when he was in school, discussions that ranged in topic from simple calculus to Devinian logic and all points in between. Yes, she was subject to the occasional bout of a philosopher's stereotypical enthusiasm for theories other scientists saw as being merely thought experiments. But Baraq had grown to appreciate her wisdom and her reason. A calmness enveloped her that made everything she did seem important. All of this—her wisdom, her reason, and her calmness—had led Baraq to give her the strange mechanism he had found embedded in the device.

"I wasn't sure what to suspect," he said, finally answering her question.

"But you *did* suspect?"

Baraq nodded.

Louratna pursed her lips, then leveled her gaze. "I think the device rends space."

"Pardon me?"

"I said, I think the box tears a hole in space, connects one place with another."

Baraq laughed, feeling suddenly a bit foolish. Louratna's silent stare made him immediately uncomfortable.

"Why do you say that?" Baraq finally said.

"Dimensional breaks have been mathematically understood for nearly a cycle."

"No one believes they can exist in the real world, though."

"Experimentalists are often limited by a lack of imagination."

Baraq let the words soak in. "All right. But how do you get there from this?" He waved his hand at the box of wire and hardware.

"I will walk you through it when we have more time. But I'm convinced the system amplifies and funnels energy through its spokes. If enough energy is focused at a single point in space, singularities result."

"Singularities?"

"Holes in the fabric of the world."

Baraq shook his head. "Of what use is a hole?"

"A good question," Louratna replied. "But there's another one that comes first."

Baraq hesitated, not wanting to appear stupid. He was an engineer, after all. He should be able to follow basics. He tapped his fingers together as he considered his answer.

"How much energy would it need?"

"More than we could harness—a great deal more. But that's not the question I had in mind."

"Where would the energy come from?"

"That is the right question."

Louratna waited.

"Maybe one of the other systems on the Taranth Stone is an energy generator."

"No. Nothing on the craft could be big enough to be capable of generating that kind of energy on demand."

"Then I am at a loss," he admitted.

"Think about what is happening to our world." She waited while he thought, but nothing came. "What is our greatest source of energy?"

The answer brought him a cold chill, a touch of wrongness, something evil and dire at a level that suddenly seemed so large as to be impossible to grasp.

"Eldoro," he said. "The energy source is Eldoro."

Louratna nodded. "Do you now know the answer to your first question?"

"Which was?"

"You asked: of what use is a hole in the world?"

"To use it as a source," he said, falling back in his chair, totally overwhelmed. "The hole is inside Eldoro. It's there to take its energy."

Louratna nodded. "That interpretation matches the data."

Suddenly, everything made sense—the clouds thinning, the melting rain of acid, temperatures dropping so slowly as to be unnoticeable unless looked at over a span of time. Eldoro was dying, its heat being siphoned away. And as Eldoro diminished, their home was changing.

Baraq's hearts ached as he walked home. The night was crisp. Fresh dew sparkled with a glimmer that he once thought beautiful. He scanned the buildings along the path. Quadars slept in each. Quadars ate, and they joked with their Families, and they struggled with making the payments that kept their lives going. In between they made more Families, and they read books. In the distance, the Esgarat peaks glimmered with the light of tiny Eterdane.

His stomachs churned.

Louratna had talked further on—about a great, vast universe, about alien creatures with intelligence and vigor. About the Esgarat, their world that was dying with no way to save itself, and about other worlds—worlds filled with other beings with technologies that those here could barely imagine.

"You've got to convince your Family to work on something that will break the hole, Baraq," she had said. "We have to break the singularity or we will all die."

Baraq had no reply.

If Louratna was right, the temperature would continue to drop. The clouds would dissipate, and the burning liquid would rain down hard. It may take hundreds of years, or maybe thousands, but eventually Eldoro would be spent. Before that happened, though, the environment of their world would be a far different place and the quadarti would almost certainly be long dead.

If Louratna was right, every scientist on this world should be working to find a way to staunch the flow of Eldoro's energy through this singularity.

The councilor had been right, too. Or at least right enough.

Another mysterious set of creatures had made the Taranth Stone, but the council would never find them because they were looking in the wrong places. The world was even bigger than even Hateri E'Lar was imagining.

He stepped into his house.

"Baraq?" Crissandr's voice came from the bedchamber.

"I'm home," he called.

As he shrugged off his coat, grimacing at what the night's chill might mean, a sense of total defeat overwhelmed him.

He was getting old. Old and tired.

His world was dying, and he was powerless to change anything.

"Are you hungry?" she said from the dark doorway. She leaned against the wall, disheveled from sleep, her rounded belly bulging. "I put dinner out for you."

He walked to her and put his arms around her waist, resting his chin on her shoulder. Her smell engulfed him, and the sweet heat of her pregnant body radiated through his chest. For a moment, he saw Hara again and felt the hollow nothingness that she left inside him.

"What's wrong?" Crissandr asked after several moments.

He hesitated.

"It's nothing," he finally said.

"Don't do that, Baraq. Something's definitely wrong, and I want to know what it is."

Baraq looked at Crissandr, then. She was his pair-mate. She deserved to know, and they had already been through so much.

He slowly walked around the room, lifting pictures and examining likely positions for wave talkers. There were none. Not really surprising, he thought. Waganats were not known for bringing their business home with them, and his father wouldn't conceive of him talking to his wife about such delicate matters. Besides, his office was unoccupied long enough to ensure the wave talkers could be placed and wired, but no one could guarantee an uninterrupted time span that would be enough to wire his home.

He told her everything as he ate.

He told her about Hateri's request, about the death of two

scientists, and about wave talkers and his Family and his father. He was surprised how easily the last came, pouring like falls in underground pools, cascading, growing in power as he went, frothing and foaming with pent-up anger.

He explained what Louratna had suggested this evening.

"Your father will never work on that," Crissandr said. "There's no profit in it."

"Never," Baraq agreed. "He'll say that Louratna is a ranting-mad philosopher." He couldn't bring himself to voice his concern that his father was just as likely to kill him if he found Baraq was working on such a device.

He sat back heavily in his chair, and braced himself.

"There is something else, though."

"Yes?"

"The council has had thirty years to work on this, admittedly with poor resources, but thirty years. I've had three of the most experienced quadars I know working on it for almost an entire year."

"You're worried that even if your father takes it on as a whole, we won't be able to learn enough from it?"

"That is exactly right," he said. "At least not fast enough. What have we gotten so far, eh? A few theories and something we know is an electrical system, but wouldn't know how to build even if one of the priest's gods were to appear before us. To solve a problem with Eldoro could take generations. I don't know if we have a chance."

"That is a problem," Crissandr said. "Or a series of them. But I think you need to face them one at a time."

Baraq said nothing for a long time.

He still had no idea of exactly what he should do, but he felt better. That evening, as he slipped into an unsettled sleep, he draped his arm across the swelling form of Crissandr's belly and held her close.

CHAPTER 27

The idea was his. But Crissandr was the one who finally convinced him he should do it.

It was grasping at straws—a million-to-one against. And if his father found out, Baraq would certainly be killed. But it was all he could think of that made any sense at all. When he posed the effort to Louratna, she had her quadars shake him free of his Family watch as they had done the night of their conversation.

He stole the generator that had been stored in one of his Family's warehouses since the time of the wave talker's earliest development. It was, in fact, the very machine Jarka'el Waganat had first used to create waves all those years ago. Baraq selected it specifically because it was so old he figured no one would miss it, and because it had been modified to push waves of great power. Also because it worked in the lowest frequencies, spectrums his Family no longer monitored. The transmitter tower was built from parts he bought by depleting his accounts.

Louratna's quadars loaded the material onto a cart and drove them into the vastness of the Castanda Desert, where the wind was known to be devastating, but also where no one was around to interfere with their work. Two heats later, the power system hummed and the wave talker burst into life with electric screeches that set his teeth to rattling. He stayed an additional heat, making sure the system was operating, making sure the message was being sent out into the sky, out toward Eterdane, and then toward Katon and Eldoro.

We are here. Help us.

This simple message was sent in ragged bursts across an arching sweep of space.

Louratna ensured at least two quadars would always be staffing the transmitter, and that the message would be continually sent.

Once it was in place, Baraq packed his *tal* beast up and traveled back to his home, back to Crissandr.

The night was clear and cold when he arrived.

Crissandr smiled from their bed.

One of the nurses handed him a bundle of brown cloth that swaddled a whelpling. He took Brada—his newborn son—into his arms, felt his tiny grip, and listened to his small voice. In a moment's inspiration, Baraq carried his son out into the night and looked into a sky that was vast and clear and sprinkled with glimmering points of light.

Nothing else was there.

Nothing moving, anyway.

He closed his eyes and imagined the towering wave talker out in the dark desert, throwing its invisible waves skyward.

For maybe the first time in his life, Baraq realized he wasn't *sure* of anything anymore. He wasn't certain what he was doing, didn't know how to deal with his Family. But mostly, he realized that it didn't matter.

Small as he was, he had done what he could do.

Maybe no one was out there. Maybe the Taranth Stone had not come from another species. But maybe someone *was* out there. Maybe the quadarti were not alone.

If so, maybe these other beings could save the quadarti.

Or maybe, instead, they would be monsters and arrive only to devour the quadarti before Eldoro could burn out.

Peering into the night, he thought he saw a movement.

Or maybe it was just a trick of his eyes.

Holding his newborn son in his arms, and imagining waves that raced through the open sky, he prayed, wondering and wishing.

And hoping.

This is the end of

STARFALL

STEALING THE SUN: BOOK 3

If you enjoyed this story, you might be interested in the rest of the series:

STARFLIGHT
STARBURST
STARFALL
STARCLASH
STARBORN

If you enjoyed this story, please consider stopping by your favorite online booksellers' websites and leaving a review. Word of mouth is the most powerful force in the universe when it comes to the livelihood of your favorite authors!

ABOUT THE AUTHOR

Ron Collins is an Amazon best-selling Dark Fantasy author who writes across the spectrum of speculative fiction.

His fantasy series *Saga of the God-Touched Mage* reached #1 on Amazon's bestselling dark fantasy list in the UK and #2 in the US. His short fiction has received a Writers of the Future prize and a CompuServe HOMer Award, and his short story "The White Game" was nominated for the Short Mystery Fiction Society's 2016 Derringer Award.

He has contributed a hundred or so short stories to *Analog*, *Asimov's*, Fiction River Anthology Series, and several other professional magazines and anthologies.

He holds a degree in Mechanical Engineering, and has worked to develop avionics systems, electronics, and information technology before chucking it all to write full-time—which he now does from his home in the shadows of the Santa Catalina Mountains.

Ron's website is: www.typosphere.com
Follow Ron on Twitter: @roncollins13

Sign up for his newsletter to get free stuff!

http://www.typosphere.com/newsletter

ACKNOWLEDGMENTS

Let me start by thanking Dr. Stanley Schmidt, whose basic question "what happens next" is the reason this series exists, and who picked up a short story titled "The Taranth Stone," that is now embedded in somewhat different form in this work.

Thanks to Kevin J. Anderson for all his support, as well as his kind cover blurb about my work. Kevin was one of my earliest mentors, so it's always a blast to have his help.

Thanks also to my early readers, Chuck Heintzelman, John Bodin, and Sharon Bass.

Then, of course, there's always Lisa, who, once again, I get to thank both for her outstanding editorial hand, as well as all the other things she brings to my life every day. This book in particular carries a strong flavor of her work, and is immensely better for it.

Any issues that might remain in this work are, of course, totally on my shoulders.